Unintended Consequences

UNINTENDED CONSEQUENCES.

LARRY FONDATION

ILLUSTRATIONS BY
KATE RUTH.

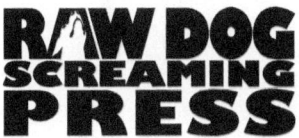

Published by Raw Dog Screaming Press
Hyattsville, MD

First Edition

Cover & Interior Illustrations: Kate Ruth
Book Design: Jennifer Barnes

Printed in the United States of America

ISBN 978-1-933293-75-2

Library of Congress Control Number: 2008944276

www.rawdogscreaming.com

Dedication

For Bett Williams: All best and love.

And special thanks and gratitude to Kate Ruth.

Also by Larry Fondation

Common Criminals: L.A. Crime Stories
Angry Nights
Fish, Soap & Bonds

Acknowledgements

Grateful acknowledgement is made to the following publications and online journals in which some of the stories in this collection were previously published, sometimes in different form:

Poetic Inhalation—"Getting Married;" *Fiction International*—"Dead Things," "Desire for Blood," "Fix," "Make Up," "Feeding the Habit," "Peacekeeper," "Loyal;" *Arcade*—"The Last Stop;" *The Brooklyn Rail*—"Central California," " The Staples Center;" *Flaunt*—"Sneaker Pimp;" *Asylum*—"Hats," "Ambulance," "Telefono;" *Two Ton Santa*—"What I Hate About the Government;" *Pleiades*—"Vietnam: The Eviction," " Baby;" *Society*—"Casper;" *Plastique*—"Hats" (revised, with Kate Ruth); *Five Fingers Review*—"Not Working;" *Pale House.com*—"Light Eater," "The Bracelet;" *Oak Square*—"The Horses of Instruction;" *Western Humanities Review*—"Thug Life."

"Not Working" also appeared, in substantially revised form, as a chapter of my novel *Fish, Soap and Bonds* (Raw Dog Screaming Press: 2007)

TABLE OF CONTENTS.

Part One
Quirks & Crimes

Part Two
Parallel Lives: Plutarch for Reality T.V.

Part Three
Working Class Heroes

PART I
QUIRKS AND CRIMES.

"Let's do it."

Gary Gilmore's last words before execution by firing squad.
Salt Lake City, Utah—1977.

Getting Married

I WAS SITTING alone at the bar. I didn't know anyone. The guy next to me was pretty big. He seemed quite drunk. He had two bottles of Heineken in front of him. The bartender took what he thought was an empty. I guess it wasn't, or maybe the guy just wanted trouble. In any case, he blamed me.

"You drank my beer."

"No, I didn't."

"Step outside and we'll settle this like men."

"Not tonight."

"What?"

"Tomorrow. I have the flu tonight."

"Fuck that."

I took out a .45 and stuck it against his head.

"I said 'tomorrow.'"

"OK," he said.

I show up the next night after 24 hours of coughing and Nyquil and Dayquil.

The guy kicked my ass.

I'm not sure if it was by accident or on purpose, but I had left my gun at home.

* * *

Two days later I came back, but he wasn't there. That's when all this really began. A mess. An awful mess. That's what I'd gotten myself into. Holed up in the bar. Well, not holed up exactly. Holding people hostage. There I said it. That's the straight scoop.

I had fifteen people in the bar and I had a gun on them. I didn't know what I was doing or why.

The cops called me.

The bartender gave me the phone.

The officer asked, "What are your demands?"

"Huh," I said.

"What do you want?" The cop had a calm voice at first, but already he was sounding impatient. He thought I was playing dumb, but I really didn't know what he was talking about at the outset.

"I need a drink," I said, into the phone, but really to no one in particular.

The cop told me to give the phone to the bartender, which I did.

"What do you want?" the bartender asked me. "I'm the owner. You can have anything you want...on the house."

I could hear the cop shouting, "hurry up" into the phone that the bartender still held to his ear. Without a hitch, the bar owner recited a list of beers. "Heineken, Corona, Amstel Light, Coors, Budweiser."

"O.K., Corona."

"You want a lime with that?"

You could hear the cop screaming into the phone, which was now sitting on the bar while the bartender opened my beer and squeezed a lime into it. I picked up the phone up off the bar and told the cop to pipe down; he was getting everyone all nervous. I told him not to try any of that 'come out with your hands up' shit and I used the owner's kindliness to suggest I had great command over the 'hostage situation,' as he had put it. Then I hung up. I mean, we were having a good time. I had about a hundred bucks in my pocket, and the place was kind of shabby, so I figured the owner couldn't be rich, so I offered to buy a round for everyone. Of course, there were only about a dozen people in the place, myself included. It was about two in the afternoon.

Then we turned on the TV to watch ourselves. I started to think about the cop's question: "What did I want?"

I think I mentioned, but maybe not, that I found one of the customers sitting there quite cute. Her name was Mariana and I loved the way she sat on the bar stool, all relaxed even when I had the gun, which I'd now handed over to the bartender, who emptied out the bullets and put the now harmless weapon back on the bar.

Of course, the cops did not know any of this. The negotiator kept calling; we'd either ignore him or pick up the phone and hang up on him, without a word.

"Fuck him," I said.

"Yeah, fuck him," Mariana said.

The next time the cop called, the owner put him on the speakerphone. "Fuck you, fuck you, fuck you!" We shouted in unison. I bought another round.

Mariana was working fourteen hours a day. Baking English muffins. One hundred thousand muffins a day. She hated it, of course.

The cop stopped calling and started using a bullhorn. Mariana put four quarters in the jukebox, and the owner turned up the volume to drown out the megaphone. It worked.

I loved hearing her stories. She loved for me to listen...

"I used to raise pit bulls with my brother," Mariana said. "We had a pretty good business going on."

"So what happened?"

"One of our dogs killed a guy, an employee of ours."

I loved hearing her stories. She loved for me to listen. She told more stories and I mostly listened, but I was so comfortable around her that I opened up to her, which I hardly ever do.

"I'm so afraid of being misunderstood," I found myself saying. "For example, a guy's car conks out. He's with his son, about ten years old. They struggle, but can't move the car. I motion like to say, 'I can give you a push with my car.' They think I want them to hurry up, that I'm waving them on, impatient-like. The guy, the father, holds up one finger, to say, like, "Just a minute," but that—hurrying—that's not what I meant at all, so you know what I mean? I was trying to be nice. But they didn't get it. That ever happen to you?"

"When do you breathe?" Mariana asked.

"What do you mean?"

"You talk fast."

"I'm nervous."

"About the cops?"

"No. About you."

"Me?"

"I want you to like me…"

She stroked my cheek. Her nails made my skin tingle and I shivered with pleasure. She pulled her hand away. "No, please," I said. I placed her hand, her nails, back up against my neck.

Meanwhile, the bar owner bought two rounds to match my two, so by now we were getting pretty lit. More cops gathered outside. The accumulated flashing blue lights were beginning to annoy us. Randy, the bartender's name was Randy- in fact, the place was called "Randy's Saloon"—anyway, Randy made doubles for Mariana and me.

"It looks like you two hit it off," he said as he passed us our drinks.

Suddenly, we heard clattering on the roof. It wasn't Santa Claus. More cops. Randy unplugged the jukebox. We took the call this time. Things were getting serious. It was a different cop on the phone this time, but he had the same question: "What do you want?"

I had to go to the bathroom.

"Randy, can you get his number?"

"Who?"

"The cop…I gotta call him back. I gotta pee."

Randy said to the cop: "He stepped out for a minute. Can he call you back?"

"What do you mean, he stepped out?" the cop shouted and then hung up.

We could all hear more footsteps and megaphones. When I got back from the bathroom, I took a deep breath. I looked Mariana straight in the eye—as best I could at least—I was so nervous.

"He stepped out for a minute. Can he call you back?"

"I want to get married,"

"What?" Mariana asked.

"Will you?"

"Yes," she said so softly I could barely hear her.

Cheers erupted from Randy and from the patrons sitting closest to us. I looked at Randy. I'd half-expected he'd let the cops in while I was in the bathroom. He noticed my nervous look.

"I wouldn't do that to you. You're getting married."

"What did she say?" an elderly patron yelled from the end of the bar.

"She said 'yes.'" Randy said. "They're getting married."

A second round of cheers went up all around—from all those who hadn't heard me pop the question.

The cops outside and on the roof were getting really worked up. The jukebox was back on full blast and you could still hear the police activity above the music.

"We've got to deal with this," Randy said, suddenly quite serious.

I looked at him blankly, though I really did understand.

"You could do 20 years," he said.

"I have an idea," the elderly man shouted, still immobile at the bar's edge.

He ambled over. It took him forever to get the ten feet to where we were sitting, but we were all ears.

"It's like a morning show," he said. "On the radio."

Mariana was biting her nails. She had great nails, long and elegant, so I moved her hand from her mouth, imagining the ring I'd slip onto her finger.

"What are you talking about?" she asked the old man.

"We'll say it was a hoax," he said. "A set up so he'd ask her to marry him—he's all shy and shit and needed the push."

"He'll still get five years," some other guy said. "Fucking with the emergency response system and shit."

"Out in a year with good behavior," Randy said.

I felt powerless in these discussions of my fate. My act was random.

"I'll marry him now and I'll wait until he gets out," Mariana said.

I kissed her. I loved her.

"We'll do it right," I said.

Randy was excited. "Let's cut a deal on the phone," Randy said. "They can get a DA on the line. We can plea bargain."

It turned out he was right. The cops were happy just to get it over with.

We were all united, so we negotiated hard.

Randy was great as the hard-ass; Mariana played the stricken bride to a tee.

I got off easy—six months, plus two years probation.

When I got out of jail, Mariana and I got married at Randy's. It was a grand affair.

Dead Things

SHE DIDN'T LIKE the dead birds and the dead rodents.

He became more direct, even pushy.

BUS # 209:

Rowena & Glendale   2:09 pm
Glendale & Glenfeliz 2:12 pm

She used high quality lipstick. She couldn't draw straight lines.

I'm a slob, he said.

The lights are out in California. On and off, really.

I'm running for Governor, she said.

Breakfast was bacon and eggs, and an English Muffin. She meant to say "dry," meaning without butter, but when the waitress came she was silent, so she got the English Muffin slathered in grease.

He had ordered for her.

I ask for money constantly.

I can never get enough…of anything.

Night-blooming jasmine penetrates the air of even the shittiest part of Los Angeles. It smells like sex, like cum on the bed covers.

I'll have a double cheeseburger, a large order of French Fries, and a Diet Coke.

I don't get around much.

Cut to the chase: Will you fuck me?

She had landscapes sketched on her tits.

Western lands and Mt. Fuji.

The trash built up on San Pedro; somehow the Department failed to collect.

I drank a lot that night—I always do.

I think of her often. Always, in fact.

Afterwards we wanted to hit the road. No car. The bus.

Greyhound terminals are both beautiful and sad.

I disembark.

Alone.

I can't live without her.

She got off at a different stop.

She was never with me.

I never watered the plants; I never minded jail. Not really.

From the observation deck, I can see the City.

I've never lived here.

Move along now, the cop said.

I move on constantly. That's not my problem.

I picked up the dead birds and the dead rats—to dispose of them.

She got so mad at me.

It didn't solve the problem.

She re-potted the plants; I still forgot to water them.

I used her lipstick to draw with—on cardboard and paper.

She got mad at me again.

Regret is the Puritan dilemma.

As always I moved on, but I never left.

The Last Stop

THE CHRISTMAS LIGHTS twinkled above the stage, above the strippers, all year round, red and green. The girls danced mostly to bad rock and roll. The bartenders, the waitresses, the dancers, the bouncer—they all were women. The place was called "The Last Stop."

Ron liked to drink alone, but not to sit alone. When he ordered from the bar, he always asked for a shot of tequila and he would always move to a table filled with people he did not know and would not talk to. They would take one look at him and stay silent.

At first Sable thought he was weird. She would avoid him even when he tipped her well, which was always.

By the fifth or sixth night, he had won some of her trust and she would let him count her tips with her—mostly ones, but sometimes a five, rarely a ten, and once, just once, even a twenty. When she got the twenty, she bent way down over the rail and deep-tongued the patron, which Ron remembered he did not like, though he had no right to care one way or another. He did think about this, analyzing the situation. But there is no accounting for jealousy.

He needed a car and she needed a car. Neither of them had one. She said she took the bus to work, and when she went out at night, her friends would give her a ride. She dropped her boyfriend six months ago. He'd been strung out on junk. He stole her money. She did pretty well dancing, she said. She was dating casually now. Nothing serious. Going to LACC. Morning classes. Sometimes it was tough to get up early when she worked until closing.

She did pretty well dancing, she said. She was dating casually now. Nothing serious...

Ron came every night, then he stopped. On purpose. After a week, he returned. Sable gave him a big hug and told him she missed him. He sat down at a table—alone this time. It was a Tuesday night, so even though he arrived late, there was still an open table. Once seated, he took out a small mirror and an electric shaver and shaved his face.

The other dancers, her friends one and all, whispered about him, but she didn't care.

Days they began to take walks, meeting just briefly for the walk, then parting company. He always wore shorts and hiking boots, no matter the season, and no matter if their stroll was merely along Hollywood Boulevard. Once they had lunch. At "Killer Burger" on the Boulevard. He paid. Just eight bucks. But it was nice of him anyhow. It's the thought that counts, you know. She said this to her friends, her fellow dancers. He thought of that ahead of time, too. He knew he was making a good impression. Despite his odd ways. He admitted those to himself. He was not unconscious of his strange behavior.

He began bringing take-out food for all the girls—winning more and more of them over each time—first pizza, then Chinese food, then a fully-catered meal. God knows how much he spent. The girls certainly didn't suspect that he'd stolen another patron's credit card—right off the bar, no one watching.

One night, she stepped outside with him. He lit up a bowl. She had never smoked weed. She giggled all through her next dance.

Another day, he met her at the Last Stop at noon. They had a drink and they had eight hours before her shift started.

"Let's go to the movies."

"Where?"

"Glendale. It's easy to get a bus."

They went to see "Pirates of the Caribbean." They talked about what a good actor Johnny Depp is and what other movies they liked.

The following weekend, Sable had to leave town to see her parents in the Bay Area. Ron housesat for her and took care of her dogs, and when she came back, the dogs were healthy and happy.

"Oh, thank you," Sable said.

"It was no trouble at all," Ron said.

"Ron, will you help me find a car?" she asked. "I've saved some money and my parents are helping me out."

The next day, Ron went out alone to find the car that Sable might buy. She had four thousand dollars. You could get something decent for that. Nothing too fancy, nothing flashy, but a few features were indispensable: a convertible top, a good stereo, leather seats, maybe power windows. An old Volvo or a Saab perhaps. Or a well-kept Buick or Mercury, maybe a late eighties model.

He took an afternoon, shopped the used car lots on Brand in Glendale. Plenty of selection. At a place called Nirvana Auto, he found a nice one: A 1989 Mercury Cougar. Perfect and a great price, too, he thought.

She was so happy when he showed it to her. She smiled and then broke into a frown.

"What's the matter?" he asked.

"It's forty-five hundred dollars and I only have four thousand."

"Go on in and bargain with him," Ron said. "Give it a try."

"What if he won't budge?"

"Then I'll give it a shot," Ron said. "Tag team, you know."

Sable went into the small hut that passed for the office of Nirvana Auto.

Ron paced outside and smoked three cigarettes.

After awhile, she came back out, a look of disappointment on her face.

"He won't go a dollar lower than $4300," she said.

Ron gave her a hug.

"I'll give it a go," he said.

"Okay," she said.

He held out his hand.

"What?" she asked.

"You gotta give me the cash."

She hesitated.

He noticed and looked hurt.

"Sable," he said, forlorn.

"Sorry," she said and handed him forty one-hundred-dollar bills.

He walked toward the office.

She started to follow him.

"Stay here," Ron said. "He already rejected your offer. I gotta go in alone."

Sable asked him for a cigarette.

"You don't smoke."

"I'm nervous," she said.

He gave her two.

Within ten minutes, he was back outside.

He had the keys behind his back. He tried to mask his success from the expression on his face.

Her eyes were open wide, looking right at him.

He tossed her the keys.

She was startled, but she brought her hands up in time and she caught the keys.

"It's all yours," he said.

Sable jumped up and down and hugged Ron and kissed him.

It was the first car she ever owned.

She cut short her glee and looked at her watch.

"Oh, shit," she said.

"What?"

"I gotta get to work," she said.

"Call in sick," he said. "It's a big day."

"I can't," she said. "I need the money. And, it wouldn't be right. It makes it hard on the other girls."

"Yeah, you're right," Ron said.

"Oh, honey," she said. "You're so wonderful."

"Let's show it off to the girls at the club tonight," he said.

"The girls will be happy for me," she said. "We've always been tight. I've been dancing with some of these girls for going on nine years."

"They'll be proud of you," he said.

"You've been so good to me," she said. "Let's go."

She jumped into the driver's seat and opened the passenger side door for Ron.

Though she was in a hurry, Sable drove carefully in her new car towards "The Last Stop."

When they got there, she couldn't find a parking space.

"I'm so late," Sable moaned.

"Go ahead and run in," Ron said. "I'll park it for you."

She looked at him with a crooked smile.

"Don't worry, I'll be careful with it."

They hugged and they kissed and she jumped out of her car and Ron climbed into the driver's seat.

She blew him a kiss over her shoulder as she ran towards the front door of the club.

Ron adjusted the seat and the mirrors and he turned the car out onto Hollywood Boulevard.

Even he felt bad when he drove off in the car, paid for with her cash, registered in his name.

He Bought Her a Ring

RICKY ISN'T FEELING particularly guilty, but a little. He hasn't slept with Donna yet, but he's smooched her. His latest in a long line of secretaries.

Real estate in Los Angeles is still good. He's made a lot of money this month. He can afford to treat Janet to something nice. They've been married a long time and she is a good wife.

He leaves work early and stops at the jewelry store. The clerk is cute and he flirts with her a little bit. He takes a long time to pick out the gift. He has the salesgirl try things on—a necklace, a bracelet, and a few different rings. Mostly diamonds, a few with other precious stones.

It is a nice store, hospitable and well lit. It is on Vermont Avenue, in the Los Feliz district. The clerk is not only cute, but friendly too. They have brandy and scotch on the counter, free for their customers. The saleswoman—her name is Stacy—offers him a drink and he accepts.

Stacy takes out a special ring—from an estate sale, she says. He likes it immediately. The ring has three stones, a sapphire and a ruby set on either side of a considerable diamond. The band is white gold.

"She'll love it," he says.

"It's a little expensive," Stacy cautions.

"I want something nice."

"It's twenty-five hundred dollars," she says.

"I'll take it," he says.

He doesn't hesitate, though he means to. He wants a nice gift, but he'd been thinking in the five hundred to a thousand dollar range.

"Should I gift wrap it?" asks Stacy

Is he secretly trying to impress the sales clerk? he asks himself. Did one glass of scotch loosen him up? Does Stacy know he feels guilty about something?

"Wrap it up, sir?" she asks.

"Oh, yes, please," he says.

Stacy wraps the ring and he pays for it—in cash. He slips her a hundred dollar tip, which she—at first—refuses, but he insists, so finally she accepts it.

They smile, a touch uncomfortably, at one another, and he leaves the store and heads home.

* * *

At their house on Franklin, Janet is cooking dinner and talking on the phone. She is chatting with their neighbor, Anne.

"You just don't like Ricky," Janet says.

"Maybe the reason I don't like him is you complain about him all the time."

"I do not," Janet says. She mixes ground meat with eggs and spices.

"That's half of what we talk about, Janet."

"You're the only one I talk to about this kind of thing."

"I'm flattered."

"Don't be a wise-ass, Anne."

Janet is peeling the skins from roasted red peppers.

"I'm just joking," Anne says.

Trying to cook and cradle the phone, Janet burns her fingers.

"Shit," she says.

"What?"

"I burned myself."

"Are you OK?"

"Yeah."

"Janet, look, I like Ricky just fine."

"I gotta go."

"Don't get pissed at me," Anne says.

"I'm not," Janet says. "But I got to pay attention. I'm cooking."

"You brought up the topic."

"I know. I know. But I still need to run. I'll call you later."

Janet puts the phone down.

She's making her husband's favorite dinner—stuffed peppers with ground lamb, not beef.

She is not finished cooking dinner when she hears the key in the lock and the door opens. Ricky is early.

* * *

Ricky has the ring box stuffed in his jacket pocket.

"Hi honey. You're early," Janet says.

"And you're cooking," Ricky says. "I was going to take you out to dinner."

"The kids are at my mother's house. I thought we'd have a nice meal at home."

"Smells great. What is it?"

"Stuffed peppers with lamb."

Ricky hugs and kisses his wife. He wants to wait for a better time to give her his gift, but he is antsy and he puts the box in her hand.

"Oh, my God. Oh, my God."

Janet forgets about Sally and about Anne and about all her complaints about Ricky, and she loves her ring, and Ricky loves her, and all their travails seem gone and they are happy right now.

* * *

After dinner, Ricky says, "Let's go out for a drink."

"I'll wear my ring," Janet says. She places it on her ring finger.

"Wanna just go down to Joey's?" Ricky asks.

"Let's go someplace special."

They go downtown, to the bar at the Bonaventure Hotel that rotates so you can see the Los Angeles skyline, such as it is.

At home, they make great love and fall asleep in one another's arms.

Janet does not call Anne back.

* * *

The next morning, Ricky gets up to go to work and Janet sleeps in before she heads to her mother's to pick up their kids. She makes herself coffee, scrambles two eggs and calls her Mom to say she'll be there in an hour.

"How are the kids?"

"They're great. They were little angels."

Janet laughs and hangs up the phone.

On her way to pick up the kids, Ricky calls.

"I just had a meeting pop up at seven," he says. "I'll be home by nine."

Janet is disappointed, but nice about it. They had such a great night last night and she is still glowing.

On her way back home from her mother's, Janet gets a call from Anne.

"Can you meet me for a drink tonight?" Anne asks.

"I've got the kids," Janet says.

"Sweetie, it's important." Anne says. Janet thinks that she sounds like she's crying.

"I'll get Arlene to come over."

Arlene is the fifteen-year-old babysitter who lives next door.

* * *

Arlene knocks on the door and the two women, young and not so young, talk about last Friday's Marshall High School football game and the sophomore quarterback Arlene likes. Arlene says her mother thinks she's too young to date. Arlene thinks fifteen is plenty old.

Janet drives to meet Anne at Joey's, their neighborhood watering hole, just off Hollywood Boulevard. The small parking lot is overflowing, so she finds a parking space on the street around the corner. Joey's is a dive, a transitional place—full of degenerates and hipsters and locals, in equal measure. But they all love it.

It turns out Anne is having marital troubles. Her husband is fooling around and, though he has apologized and has told her the affair is over, she does not know if she can forgive him. Janet notices that Anne says nothing about her ring. She wants to show it off, but she doesn't dare.

Janet listens a lot, and tries to be supportive, but as nine o'clock nears, she starts to look at her watch. She wants to get home before Ricky does.

"I don't want to keep you," Anne says.

"I'm sorry," Janet says. "I'd love to stay and talk. I know how upset you are, but Arlene has homework and I told her I'd be home by eight-forty-five."

"I understand, of course," Anne says.

"I'll buy your drinks," Janet says. She puts thirty dollars on the table.

"You go," Anne says. "I think I'm going to stay for one more, fortify myself before I go home."

Anne stuffs the money in her purse.

Janet leans over the table and kisses Anne on the cheek. Anne reaches up to hug her.

"You're sure you're O.K?"

"I'm fine," Anne says. "Thank you. You're a great friend."

"I'll call you tomorrow," Janet says.

Janet rushes out, and thinking only of getting home quickly, she is particularly unaware of her surroundings.

The street she is parked on is especially dark.

She is walking fast; she does not hear footsteps.

When she feels the tug on her purse, she reacts; she draws her arm to her chest. She does not scream.

The mugger grabs her shoulder and spins her around. He has a knife.

Janet understands the knife. She holds out her purse, extends it towards him as if she were giving him a present.

Apparently he notices the gleam of her new ring under the only streetlamp.

Recognizing value when he sees it, he now scoffs at the offer of the purse.

With his knife at Janet's throat, he drags her off into the dark of an alley. Once in the cover of the alley, he wrenches Janet's finger, trying to pull off the ring.

"No, please," is all Janet manages to say.

She makes a fist. The mugger tries to pry her fingers open. Janet resists.

He begins to hack at her hand with his knife.

Now she opens her hand. But then she makes a fist again. He continues slashing her hand. It is unclear whether she is trying to save her ring or trying to minimize the surface her assailant can cut.

It doesn't matter. He is lost now inside his own desire—now it is both for the ring and for her blood.

Janet strikes him in the face, which only makes him madder.

He makes short work of it now: he pins her to the ground; he uncurls her fingers; he cuts her finger off and quickly scoops up the ringed finger and puts it in the pocket of his jeans.

The mugger runs away.

* * *

Janet scrambles back to Joey's. She is surprised at how little pain she feels.

Anne is still there, drinking. "Oh, my God," she says.

Janet is mostly silent.

On the way to the hospital, Janet insists on calling Ricky. She does not have her cell phone because the mugger stole her purse as well. Anne dials the number and hands Janet her phone.

Janet tells Ricky she is all right, and that she is on her way to the hospital, but that is all she says.

"You left it all out," Anne says.

"Leave me alone," Janet says.

She does not want to talk about the whole story. She does not want to talk, or to tell any story at all.

It is only when he arrives at Hollywood Presbyterian Hospital that Ricky learns the whole story about what has happened, that both the ring and her finger are gone.

Cabron

"Cabron…

"Cabron.

"Cabron!"

Jesse said the word louder each time.

The bar was dark and not crowded.

Jose looked around to see who was talking to who.

Jesse tried to get under a light so he'd be clearly seen.

"After he'd said "Cabron" for the fourth time, this time shouting, Jose approached him.

"You talking to me?"

"Who the fuck are you? De Niro?" Jesse asked, mocking.

"Are you calling me 'cabron,' asshole?"

"No, man. I wouldn't call you 'cabron.'"

"I didn't think so."

Jose turned around to walk away, feeling triumphant.

Jesse had a book tucked under his arm.

He spoke again: "…That's because you're a fucking pinche pendejo…"

Jose turned again and pulled out a gun.

"Come on, man," Jesse said. "You need that? Let's step outside: mano a mano, ese."

Jose waved the gun around. But his face lacked color.

"Put the gun down, vato," Jesse said. "Let's go outside and fight."

Jose continued to wave the gun around and Jesse continued to taunt him.

"You don't need no gun, man…do you?"

Jose hesitated, stepping forward towards Jesse and then back. Finally he fired his gun at the ceiling and shouted:

"Don't fuck with me!"

The security guards, well armed, came and tossed Jose out the door, but did not arrest him.

Jose skulked home, the guards jeering him as he walked away.

Jesse stayed another hour-and-a-half until closing.

He and his friends had a good laugh.

He tried to pick up Marisela, the best-looking woman at the bar, but she turned him down.

After the bar closed, Jesse went straight home. He was walking up his front stairs when gunshots cut into his torso.

At the hospital, the doctors pronounced him paralyzed for life from the neck down.

No one was ever charged with a crime.

Central California

We stopped in Delano but avoided the politics. Instead we talked about the Dodgers and the Giants.

We stayed in a shack with an old friend who worked in the fields. Don brought home a hooker. You had to piss outside and she didn't like that so she pissed on Don. Don didn't mind, but our friend got angry. He said his wife was sleeping. We said we didn't know he was married, but he threw us out in the middle of the night anyway. We slept in the car.

I organized cannery workers in Stockton for twelve years. I worked for the Teamsters. For the last six months, I'd been unemployed. Don and I met in Fresno, in August, on a day when it was a hundred and twelve. We'd been traveling together for three months.

The next morning we drove south. The roads were slick with oil. We watched a truck crash through the center divider and turn over.

After that we stopped for a beer. We had driven only twelve miles.

In the bar there were scores of cats and dogs and some men and a few skinny women.

"Take one of these dogs, will you?" asked a bleached-blonde woman with buck teeth and decent tits.

"We're on the road," I said.

A big guy with a beer forced a scrawny black dog on Don at gun point. Don told me later he did the guy in the men's room. He said it wasn't coerced, just a friendly blow job.

We put the dog in the car and drove away in a dust storm.

In Bakersfield we visited a carnival. The freak show wasn't much. There was a guy with three arms, but so what.

The rides were okay.

Don tried to pick up a man with tattoos and a mustache. The man was running the roller coaster. Don struck out, but the guy was nice about it. He told Don not to take it personally. My pal Don settled instead on a sixty year old red-headed woman in a tank top. He did her behind the fun house.

"Sex is sex," Don said.

In the meantime, I was celibate as a priest. I hadn't gotten any since we left Portland.

Don won a big, stuffed dog by throwing wooden rings around a bowling pin about eight feet away. We put the new dog in the car with the old dog and the first dog ripped the second one apart. The carny's dog had real bones and teeth. It was the real thing, a St. Bernard, stuffed by a local taxidermist named Doctor Breaux. We looked it up in the phone book. He was the only guy listed.

I drove fast. The white lines dividing the road flicked like strobe lights. I took another sip of Southern Comfort.

The doctor served us tea. He stood behind his product. He gave us a new dog, this time a Great Dane. Our dog still snarled at it. We gave our dog to the doctor. An even trade. We got back in the car.

"I want to see Lucy," I said.

Don agreed.

We headed straight for Pacoima.

We stopped for gas in Lost Hills.

The car almost died on the Grapevine. The Great Dane came in handy. We ate at Stuckey's and at Denny's. That was all the money we had.

The road curled through the mountains like Shirley Temple's hair. I like old movies. I let Don know what I like. I can talk to Don about things like that.

At dawn we took a spin around the Tom Bradley landfill. The dump wasn't open yet. There was a guy sitting on top of the trash heap. He looked like Buddha. Of course he did—you know, cross-legged and all. Don said he was Buddha. Lucy laughed. She said we could stay at her place or take her to a Motel 6. Her brother was home.

The next morning Don and I headed out north again—by ourselves, two buddies, driving to Delano.

One good thing—we hadn't seen a cop in over a week.

A truck crashed where the Five and the Ninety-Nine split. It was filled with chickens. They all escaped. Unscathed, it seemed. It had started all over. Just like before. It would be six months before I made it down to see Lucy again.

Desire for Blood

I WANTED TO kill somebody real bad, but I didn't want to do any time. I had to come up with a plan. It would have to be self-defense. I thought about my options.

To conceal a gun, I'd need a coat. Not cold enough—especially in Los Angeles. I'd have to wait until winter. I couldn't wait that long. And, besides, carrying a concealed weapon is itself a felony—no matter the circumstances. I couldn't contrive a circumstance that I could explain.

Stabbing or clubbing some one was out of the question. Too messy, for one, and, too dangerous as well. I'm a small guy—five-five and skinny. Poisoning a person. No. Too distant. Too British. I'm not an Agatha Christie fan. It had to be somewhat visceral. But visceral for a guy weighing a hundred and thirty? Come on. Who am I kidding?

Out on a walk one night, just off Sunset, near Echo Park, I spied part of my answer. A martial arts studio.

"Do you teach deadly force?" I asked.

"Yes," the teacher assured me. "But, more important, we teach how to avoid the use of force at all."

"Of course," I answered.

I knew this was the place.

I got real good real fast. Yellow belt, brown belt, then black. Within 60 days. I was a natural, the teacher said. Of course I didn't tell him I'd done some of the basics in the Army. My past was my secret; my pension kept me alive. I did this stuff ten hours a day. Seven days a week. When the studio was closed on Sunday, I worked out at home.

OK. Now I was an expert. A black belt with a couple of stripes. Enough to do the trick. Now what? I couldn't just go out and chop some one in the neck while I was walking down the street. I still wanted to. All that meditation hadn't tamed my desire one bit.

I came up with a great idea. I bought a wheelchair. I faked an accident. I went straight to a crime-infested neighborhood. I had plenty to choose from. I picked Pico-Union. Time: a little after two in the morning. Bars getting out. People getting rowdy. Chances were that I'd get accosted. Plenty of justification on its way.

The first night, nothing happened. A couple of Salvadoran guys gave me quarters. They assumed I was homeless.

The next night, I went to Compton. I didn't quite know where to go and I found myself sitting amidst a bunch of warehouses. I didn't see a soul. I had to take a cab back. I couldn't find the bus route. I wasn't taking my car. If my vehicle was parked in the neighborhood of the justifiable homicide, it would raise questions, hurt my credibility. I'd always planned to say I got lost on the bus. I took the bus because I couldn't drive. I couldn't drive because of my injury. That's how my story would go.

The third night I went to Boyle Heights. Nothing. I was frustrated that I couldn't get trouble to come my way. The newspaper headlines had been blaring murders for a decade. I couldn't even attract a mugger.

The fourth night I decided to take the evening off. Go to a movie. I went to Beverly Hills. A special screening. A French film. Godard. No, not "Breathless." I still took the bus. I didn't want to do anything out of the ordinary.

When the movie let out, I took out my wallet. Not for that reason, I swear. I'd been sitting on it the whole night, and the film was kind of long, the way those European movies are, and I was uncomfortable. That was my only motivation. Of course, I was jumped from behind. Instinctively, I leapt from my chair and started waling on the guy. He never knew what hit him. Within two moves, I broke his neck. My fourth shot slammed his nose through his brain and he died on the spot. Not in the ambulance on the way to the hospital. Not DOA in the ER. But immediately. You didn't need a paramedic or a doctor to tell you the guy was gone.

The shit of it is that, during the court proceedings, during which I was pretty quickly exonerated, the guy's story came out. It was straight out of Les Miz, which I never did see while it was playing here in LA. You know the story: the guy gets thrown in jail for stealing bread. Well, get this, the guy I killed, he was trying to pull together money for an operation for his younger brother. Or maybe his mother, anyway, some close family member; I don't remember the details. But you get the point. He wasn't some murderous son of a bitch, but a tragic case. A sob story.

They let me go anyway, of course. A mugging's a mugging. He started it. Even if it was for a good cause, so to speak. I got a doctor to testify for me. The guy's lawyers asked—a reasonable question, I guess—that if I was so hurt, how did I leap from my chair to deliver lethal blows? Smartly, my doctor compared me to old ladies who can lift cars if a loved one is pinned underneath. You know, adrenaline flow, and super-human strength under extreme conditions. He went on at great length and in fine detail. He was extremely convincing. I was nodding my head vigorously in agreement in the court room, almost forgetting he was talking about me.

It's been five years. I've thought of confessing. But what good would it do? It wouldn't bring the guy back. You hear that all the time. And, there's a lot of truth to it. I have done something positive though. Made lemonade out of lemons, if you will. I'm making my contribution to society. I started a group called "Self-Defense Killers Anonymous." Yeah, I know, we need to work on the name. But the LA chapter alone now boasts nearly two hundred members. And, we've got groups up and running in ten major cities around the country. I hear through thee grapevine that the Japanese are latching onto us big time, too. The groups are amazing. They really are. We've got this one jeweler on Doheny. He's blown away six guys—six different incidents. Some of the accessories got away, but never the principals. All six of them, stone dead. The guy tells his story at least every other meeting. No one ever gets tired of it. It's the best story and we all love it. He cries at just the right times, but if you look closely enough—and you have to see him eight, ten times to catch it—you can see just a slight smile as he puts the finishing touches on the tale.

Fix

NEITHER OF US has either money or time. I threw my life away (wife, kids, job) about five years ago, and I am trying not to care—about anything. The problem is: when I get sentimental, I get violent. Always have. And frequently, too. Like pretty much every-day. With family, with friends, with perfect strangers. In my business, I stay alive when I'm violent, but still I try to keep things at a minimum because I know myself. Now, at this moment, I am just trying to relax and go about my business without a fuss.

Right this minute, she wants crack; I want a blowjob. Right now this is all that mat-ters. I've never seen this woman before, but she kneels in front of me and I pull out my cock and I stuff it in her mouth, and her two year-old son is standing behind her and is pulling on her hair and saying, "Mommy," over and over, and her apartment is filthy, and I cannot get hard, but not because of the kid or the filth, and when I pull my dick out of her mouth, I stick the crack pipe into it, and she looks up and smiles, grasping the pipe with her hands, and her hands are the only beautiful thing in the room, her nails dirty, but long and elegant anyway—her nails must be naturally strong to stay that length—so I push her head away and place her hands on my cock and she strokes it and I get very hard and her son is pulling her hair, but she doesn't seem to notice, so I close my eyes so I don't see all the broken things and her ragged long nails catch my skin from time to time, and I wince, but I like it, so I get harder and then I come in her hand. I'm happy, so I give her a couple of rocks, and I pat her son on the head, and I hand him five dollars though he's not old enough to know what money is, but fuck it, and his mother is still kneeling in front of me, and I stroke her cheek, and I have some place else to be, so I just zip up and walk out the door, and I say, "See you tomorrow."

Sneaker Pimp

I began not to like my job.
Selling sneakers. Stolen ones.
At first I just shoplifted them,
a pair here and a pair there—
supplementary income, if you
will. Then I made a friend at
the train yards. He got palettes
full. I had to split the profit with him, but the volume more than made up for it with respect
to my income. My percentage return was down, of course, but 100% of twenty or thirty
bucks is never very much. At our peak, we were hitting three thousand a week. When
Reggie got busted off loading a boxcar, I lost my supplier.

In the meantime, I'd acquired an expensive girlfriend. Her name was Merry. She didn't
want just a purse; she wanted a Prada. She didn't just want heels; she wanted Manolo Blahnik.
I had no idea who or what these things were until I saw my credit card bills. She was a great
fuck, and all my friends were jealous because she was so fine. I had to keep her.

So I started driving to the suburbs and mugging rich kids. I never had to use force.
The little snot-nosed bastards, even the football players, all gave up without a fight.
At first all I took were their shoes. After all, I was in the shoe business; it was the only
business I knew. But then I figured that if some one would surrender a hundred-fifty
dollar pair of Air Jordans without so much as a peep of protest, it must be easy come,
easy go. So anyway I started asking for their wallets. To my pleasant surprise, these
kids carried a lot of cash, too. When the police in these sleepy hollows—Monrovia, La
Canada, places like that—began extra patrols, I'd move on. LA's a big place.

Business was so good and Merry so demanding that I had to expand. I began to hire
and train associate muggers. Soon I had a dozen efficient robbers, trained in persuasive, non-
violent threats. I dispatched them north and south—Lompoc, Solvang, Carlsbad, La Jolla.

Though I bought her more and more things, Merry left me for a real estate broker
working Malibu. No offense to me or my booming business, she said. Just that I was
spending way too much time at work, and not enough with her. I wasn't sad. There
were plenty of girls now, though I missed being domestic, coming home to a woman
and a martini or a glass of Chardonnay, acting married.

Nine months into full operation we had an accident. Arnie, a sweet kid really, and one of my fastest employees, got resistance. He held firm to our business principles. He didn't fight back. Instead he got the shit beat out of him by an offensive tackle from Montecito.

Arnie was OK, and I gave him ten grand in lieu of workers' compensation, but I took it hard. Harder than he did, psychologically at least. He was back on the streets in two weeks. He had the jitters, he said, for the first two or three jobs. Then he steadied himself and was good as new. Meanwhile, I became insomniac.

We developed internal conflict within the organization. I had to promote some one to be my right-hand, and I'd picked Ralph. Wrong guy. Ralph wanted to expand into Gardena, Santa Fe Springs, places like that. I was afraid we'd get our asses kicked. I was right. We had two guys stabbed within a week. Plus, I had vowed I didn't want anything from anyone who had to work for it. No poor kids, not even middle class. Only rich kids.

I could've handled Ralph if I had a mind to, and I'm not just bragging. There wasn't much to the guy really. Just a lot of noise. But, I hesitated—not just with Ralph, but with the whole shebang. I'm not sure why—even now. But I knew I'd lost it. I lost it all, my will, my nerve, my get-up-and-go.

Ralph took advantage and quickly consolidated his position. Revenue went up. We had higher losses, but greater volume more than made up for the setbacks. I resigned without a fight.

About a month later, I was getting into my car after a stop at the 7-11 on Barrington. (Yes, I lived in Brentwood; I still had a tidy sum saved from my days as the head honcho.) As I was closing my door, I was accosted by a young man—couldn't have been more than 18—wearing an orange and green uniform; he looked like a maintenance man, a janitor, or delivery man. Maybe Sparklett's Water. He had a gun. We'd never used weapons of any kind.

"Give me your money and your shoes," he said.

I removed my British Knights and handed them over to him. He looked down his nose at them, but stuck them in his bag anyway.

"Come on, come on," he said. "Hurry up." He did not say "please," but, then again, he did not curse either.

I handed him my wallet.

He took out the cash, nearly a thousand dollars—I don't know why I was carrying so much money—and gave me back the wallet itself, my credit cards, etc. undisturbed, and safely inside. Still good policy.

As he turned to go, I spoke: "Say hi to Ralph," I said, nonchalantly and therefore certain I would shake him up.

"Ralph?" he said in all sincerity. "Who's Ralph?"

Hats

SHE WORE THE hat and he loved the hat but then he took it off her head and put it on his own and she protested but to no avail. He ran off with the hat and she proffered her pain but went immediately to his drawers to even the score, donning one of his favorite shirts, which she could wear, essentially, as a dress, although she was skeptical about wearing it in public but she did anyway thereby showing great daring.

All her friends told her the dress looked fine on her, that J. Crew and Banana Republic and all the other classy places in Pasadena sold shirt-dresses all the time and that this one looked no different; furthermore they asserted their understanding of her deep pain, her sense of loss.

She wore the shirt-dress everyday for fear if she took it off even to wash it he would get it back; and, because she didn't like the smell that was starting to accrue nor the stains that seemed to gather she began to try to wash it while it was still on her body finally resorting to taking a shower while still wearing it and then sitting in the sun to dry off. This necessitated her getting up extremely early in the morning for the process was very lengthy. For the longest time, she did not see again her man or her hat, the one he and she had both once so loved, so imagine her surprise when on the 143rd day of her wearing the shirt-dress the police showed up at her office with a warrant for her arrest for the larceny of the shirt and when she tried to counter-complain about the loss of her hat the police responded by saying there was no proof that such a hat existed now or ever whereas about the shirt there was no doubt since she was wearing it on her body and since it was easily recognizable, the man's name having been stitched into the collar, his monogram into the sleeve, both at her suggestion, she noted as she as escorted into the waiting police car.

Where I Am Right Now

I was supposed to shoot him, but I chickened out. It turned cloudy when I expected it to be clear. Outside, that is. Right now I am in Florida, or rather that is where I am supposed to be.

I listen to Steve Miller, have since the 70's, until the other day this guy comes up to me—a guy I hardly know—and says, AYou should be listening to some one else; it's the 90's now. I bought some CD's the next day, new bands—Guns 'N Roses, The Smiths, Nirvana—but I'm not so sure. I still go back to Space Cowboy.

The Cheezits are gone and I am hungry.

I am not going to get paid; I know that.

She is pretty and blonde and she is sitting next to me, painting her toenails.

"Are you waiting for the flight to Miami?" I ask.

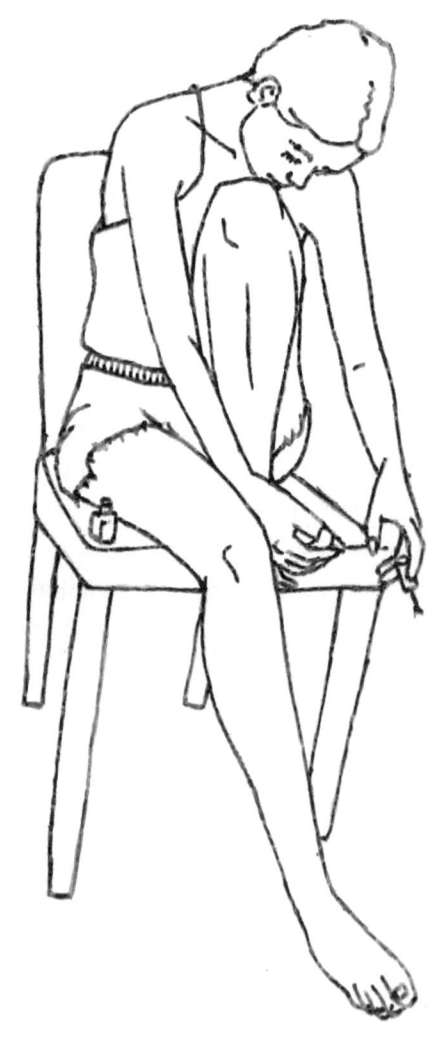

"Yes," she answers, politely, without looking up from her nails.

The color is fluorescent orange. I tell her that I like it, and she asks me to blow on it so that it dries while she does the other foot. She is in a hurry, and wants to finish her toenails before boarding the flight, so I do it for her. I find myself getting hard. My lips are very close to her foot. When they call the flight, she leaves. I do not. I wave to her, feebly it seems to me.

I am 37 years old, six foot two, with dark brown hair. I have never in my life held a steady job and I have lived in Torrance, CA, since I was thirteen. I've had two wives and about six steady girlfriends—that's it—I'm not much into one-night-stands.

My apartment in Torrance is very tidy. I keep everything clean and in its place. I have a complete collection of National Geographic magazines, dating back to 1971. Every volume, every issue.

I cannot go back to my apartment. I cannot go back to California. I know that.

I have never broken the law. This was a dumb idea in the first place. I got the blonde's phone number, but I throw it away, right there in the airport. It doesn't make any sense. Not now.

For some reason I think of the opening of Caesar's Gallic Wars: "All of Gaul is divided into three parts." I learned it in high school in Latin, "Omnia Gallia en tres partes divisa est." I have never forgotten it. However, I remember no pieces of worldly wisdom, though I must have learned something along the way.

Right now I am at the airport in Atlanta thinking about what to do next, wondering, staring at the ceiling.

The time is now. There is no later. Planes come and go. I remain where I am right now.

What I Hate about the Government

THERE ARE THESE weeds, you know, right by the freeway exit near my apartment. On a big hill where the ramp comes down, where you see the prisoners picking up litter sometimes and sticking it in big orange bags.

I've got bad allergies, but the government doesn't give a shit. I call and call. They don't do a fucking thing about the weeds.

When I was holed up at the bank—the police cars surrounding the building—I threatened to shoot my way out. It was hard to convince them that I didn't want any money.

PART II

PARALLEL LIVES:

PLUTARCH FOR REALITY T.V.

"...the most glorious exploits do not always furnish us with clearest discoveries of virtue or vice in men; sometimes a matter of less moment, an expression or a jest, informs us better of their characters and inclinations..."

Plutarch, *The Life of Alexander the Great* (translated by John Dryden)

1a. Make-Up

SHE WAS STANDING at the mirror, putting on make-up. I came up behind her. She saw me, but she did not see the knife I held in my hand. But then, I never saw the gun she kept in her cosmetics drawer, right next to the lipstick, the eyeshadow, the bottles of nail polish.

1b. Feeding the Habit

ON STAGE AT the Starlight, Amber shoots up while she strips. She is, as the saying goes, all skin and bones. Her non-tits end in pierced nipples. Her hair is short and bleached past blonde with black roots. Her thighs are thin as fork tines. The guys love her. They slip dollars, sometimes tens and twenties, under the tourniquet she straps around her arm. They applaud madly when she hits a vein. They sigh and slump in their chairs when her song ends and she has to leave the stage.

2a. Cop Story: Teddy Bears

IT WAS NEAR Pershing Square. Two days before Christmas. Proposition 187 had just passed in California, bringing tons of shit down on innocent immigrants. The man was selling Teddy Bears, giant ones, cheap ones, stuffed with newspapers—just trying to make a living.

I was picking up something—who remembers what—at the drugstore, a Thrifty or a Sav On, some chain or other.

The cops came in some Dragnet move—unmarked cars mixed with black and whites. I thought the man had sewn drugs inside the stuffed animals. No, not at all. They were busting him for selling without a peddler's license.

2b. Homeless Suite: Nevada

HE WAS STANDING outside the Desert Inn. I gave him a dollar. He went inside and fed it to a slot machine. I waited and watched. He played the machine nearest the door. He lost. Within a minute, he was back outside, asking again. Two or three people, variously dressed from preppy to slinky, brushed him off. I was only a few yards away. I walked over to him again. Recognizing me, he took a step backwards and almost fell over. I reached out to steady him, grabbing him by the arm. I felt the material of his shirt sleeve, pure silk I was certain. But, what the hell. I gave him the ten dollars I held in my other hand.

3a. Peacekeeper

THE NUN WAS watching both of us.

She had been sent by an international relief agency.

It was cold, much colder than I was used to. I had lived in California for a long time, in Los Angeles.

Now I was a United Nations peacekeeper.

The other captive was our captor's enemy.

I was neutral. The nun was there to make sure there were no atrocities. Our captor did not care about the nun.

He handed me a knife.

He pointed at his enemy and he looked at me.

"Peacekeeper, stab him right now or I will shoot both of you," he said.

I declined.

The captor shrugged.

He made the same proposition to his enemy, that he should kill me or we both would die. Though we had never spoken, the other man, our captor's enemy, refused as well.

Our captor then shot the nun.

"You didn't say anything about the nun," the enemy of our captor said.

The captor then shot him.

I braced myself.

"Keep the peace," the captor said and then he walked away, leaving me with the corpses of his enemy and the nun.

I sat there and shivered in the cold with the two dead bodies.

3b. Loyal

THEY HAD PLANNED it for a long time and, from the beginning, Brian knew that what they were doing was just.

When the day came, it was overcast, odd for the time of year. At dinner Brian was tense. The family talked about the weather, then laughed at how silly the discussion had been, given all that was going on. Their dinner table conversation was usually lively with the issues of the day.

* * *

The bomb was hidden in a basket of laundry. They wheeled a cart full of dirty clothes into the basement of the Ministry. No one was watching. All that remained was the task of setting the timer. Then they could leave and watch the place go up. Read about their work the next day in the papers.

Brian reached under the clothes to set the timer. He fumbled beneath the linens.

"What's the matter?" James asked. "Everything all right?"

"Yes, yes," Brian said. "Fine."

They peeled off their stolen uniforms as they made their way to the exit door. James was giddy with excitement.

James said, "We've done it. We have helped the cause."

"Come on, now. I'll buy you a beer," he added, slapping Brian on the back. "We deserve it."

They walked out of the targeted building towards a local pub.

Brian had the bomb shoved down under his pants, the timer still ticking the way he had set it. He could feel it thumping against his crotch, nine minutes still to go. He walked slowly with James along the deserted street.

4a. Adoption Fair

THEY TOOK THE kids from the group home and set them up in booths at the park.

The grown-ups circled round and round and checked out the children.

It was overcast, but warm—early October in Los Angeles. The supervisors made the kids bring raincoats and umbrellas, just in case.

The kids, mostly boys, were Black and Latino; the visiting adults were almost all white.

Susan and Al had picked out a puppy at the pound the day before. They brought the dog with them to the adoption fair.

Susan carried the tiny dog in her arms. She had put a bright green sweater on the dog and she had it swaddled in blankets.

They were the only couple that had brought a dog and the kids loved the dog.

Daryl had had a dog when he lived with his parents. Then his parents began to do drugs and got divorced, but fought anyway because they couldn't stay apart, and then the police and Children's Services came into their home and put his mother and his father in jail and Daryl and his brother and their dog were all separated and scattered and Daryl was five then and now he was eight and he had never seen any of them ever again, though they always told him they would try to reunite his family.

Susan took the dog from booth to booth and the kids played with the dog and Susan asked questions of the staff, and of a few of the kids, and Al was mostly quiet, but he wanted to adopt a kid, too.

When they reached Daryl's booth, he was the 9th kid they'd seen, and, more than any other kid, he fell in love with the dog.

The feeling was mutual and the dog jumped from Susan's arms into Daryl's arms and the dog licked Daryl's face and Daryl laughed.

Susan nudged Al and Al asked Daryl's name—they hadn't asked any other kids' names, though they all were wearing nametags—and Daryl said, "Daryl."

The supervisor assigned to Daryl smiled and nodded and felt encouraged.

Daryl and Susan and Al talked for a long time, and the whole time—maybe half-an-hour—Daryl held the dog in his arms, and then the Adoption Fair was over.

"Is it OK?" Susan said to Al and he knew what she meant, though no one else did.

Susan turned to the supervisor.

"Can he keep the dog?" she asked.

Daryl rose to the balls of his feet.

The supervisor said—warmly but clinically—as if she'd rehearsed the line, though she had not: "There are no pets allowed in the children's group home."

"Oh," Susan said.

"Here's my card," the supervisor said. "If you want to follow up."

"Oh, yes," Susan said. "Thank you." She took the woman's card.

The attendees at the fair all went to their different homes, and the kids went back to the same place they always did.

Susan and Al never called back.

"There are no pets allowed in the childrens group home."

4b. Vietnam: The Eviction

I HAD LED a rent strike at their run-down building. Thirty-two units of total disgrace.

Mrs. Roberts was the vocal leader.

Her husband had fought in Vietnam, and then, like so many others, he had gone crazy.

She took their four kids and moved into a cheap apartment.

There were rats and there were roaches and then the heat went off and it was Boston, and it was winter, and then I came along, and the tenants went on strike

I can remember talking with Mrs. Roberts in her living room and we discussed tenants' rights and the state of the world.

Mrs. Roberts saw some connection—her husband went nuts in Vietnam and most of her new neighbors were Vietnamese.

She was 40 and attractive, beautiful, even with bad teeth and bitten nails.

She talked a lot about Vietnam and about her neighbors.

I remember so clearly. She always dropped the 'N' in Vietnamese—"Viet-tamese."

When she got her eviction notice, she wouldn't budge, wouldn't move.

Eventually the landlord sent a goon squad, accompanied by marshals.

As they took her furniture from her apartment and put it into the street, Mrs. Roberts shouted and protested, but she stayed calm.

Her youngest daughter was two at the time.

When—last of all—they moved her baby's crib onto the sidewalk, she lost it.

The marshal tried to restrain her.

"Calm down," he said," "Lady, calm down."

I was there the whole time.

At that point, I spoke up.

"Hey, pal," I said. "If somebody was putting your kid's crib on the street, would you be calm?"

He let go of Mrs. Roberts.

When all of officialdom left, I stayed standing there with her and her kids, feeling I don't know what.

I made some calls.

Within a few minutes, the staff from a local family shelter came and picked them up.

I stayed with the furniture for an hour or two. No one came for it, of course. I didn't know what to do. The sun went down and I went home.

5a. Staples Center

DURING THE SEASON of cold and rain—January and February in Los Angeles—Carlos crawled into the dumpster behind Las Manzanitas apartments to sleep.

He usually went to bed around midnight, walking over to the relative quiet of Francisquito Way after a night of drinking with his friends by the LA River.

The tenants at Las Manzanitas liked Carlos. When they took their trash down in the morning they would always knock, and they would knock gently, so as not to jar him, and they would wait until he climbed out, and they would chat together, and he would help them throw their bags into the dumpster and together they would tidy up the parking lot and the areas and yards around their building. They spoke to one another in Spanish and in English and after the morning routine, Carlos would move along, heading to the Midnight Mission for a meal.

The disposal company truck came once a week, on Thursdays, to empty the giant receptacle that Carlos slept in. They came very early, at six in the morning. Carlos was not an early riser. The tenants told Carlos of the schedule, and they warned the drivers that Carlos was inside so they could wake him before they hoisted the dumpster's contents into their truck.

For a time, it all worked out.

Soon however, bulldozers appeared all around Las Manzanitas apartments, razing structure after structure until the building stood nearly alone, flattened earth and rubble all surrounding it and dust rising always in the air to the movements of heavy equipment.

Shortly after the arrival of the demolition and construction crews, the tenants got their eviction notices and their official letters outlining the relocation assistance they would receive.

The new sports arena needed the land that Las Manzanitas rested on for parking and the building had been sold.

The morning after the letters were delivered the tenants talked with Carlos about their impending move.

"I guess I'll go when you do," he said.

The next day was Wednesday, not Thursday. The new owners of Las Manzanitas, who would tear the building down within three months, had their own disposal contractor and had fired the old company, not wanting two. No one had seen a need to inform the tenants of the change in schedule. The disposal truck with its metal arms for hoisting and its compactor to conserve space and create efficiency arrived at six.

Carlos awoke as his dumpster turned upside down and the contents poured into the truck. The truck was noisy and the driver could not hear Carlos' screams. As he always did, the driver counted to ten and activated the compactor.

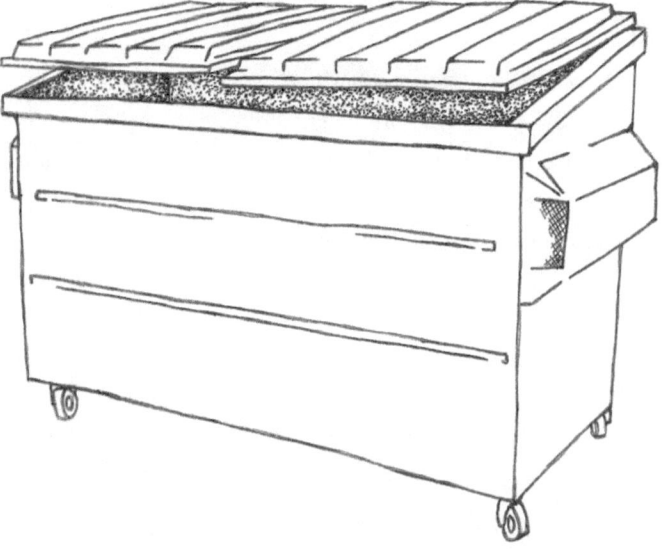

5b. Strolling

J.L. Hill walked south on Figueroa. About thirty yards ahead strolled a woman (probably Latin judging from her olive skin) in a very short black skirt and high-heeled sandals. Her legs were sturdy, solid, but so shapely—gorgeous, in fact. Hill picked up his pace. Against a flashing "Don't Walk" signal, the woman trotted across 7th street, her heels clicking rapidly on the pavement with each short, quick step. Hill started to run to catch up, but not so fast to catch her attention. He missed the light.

Hill was short and fat and sweating now, but he made up a great deal of ground between 7th and 8th Streets. At 8th he hit the jackpot. Miss Legs was stopped cold by the flow of westbound traffic, as closely spaced as a string of Christmas lights. She couldn't have jaywalked with a tank, he thought. Hill sauntered up besides her, trying not to breathe too hard.

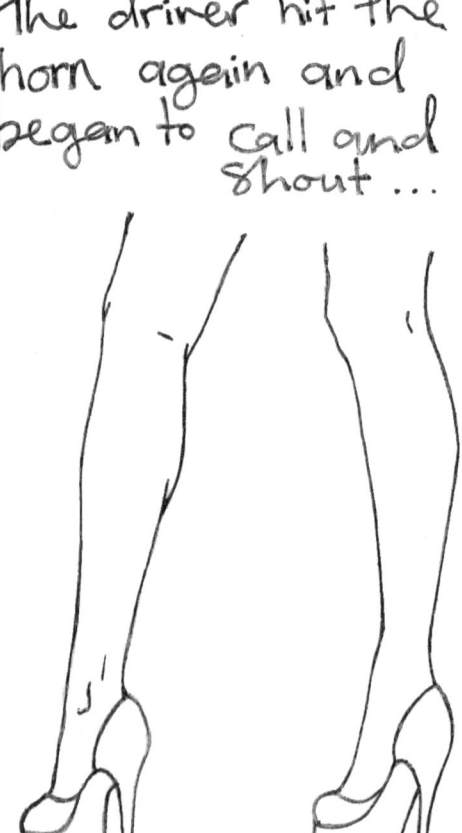

The driver hit the horn again and began to call and shout ...

A new red Mustang convertible pulled to the curb. The driver, a blond man with a pony tail and a scraggly beard, honked and whistled and let out a howl.

Miss Legs did not turn her head.

The driver hit the horn again and began to call and shout: "Fuck me, baby."

"Go fuck yourself, you scaggy-looking bastard," Miss Legs hollered back.

"You got a nice ass, baby. I'll stick you good."

"Fuck off, loser," the woman said. "I'd rather fuck him." She pointed at J.L. Hill. (She meant no harm.)

The man in the Mustang did not miss a beat. He pulled out a Colt Python and pointed it at Hill. He squeezed off three shots in a short burst, then another short burst, all right on target. Hill slumped to the ground.

The downtown lunch crowd scattered screaming. The driver persisted.

"He's dead. Will you fuck me now?"

Miss Legs made for the convertible, hurdling over the closed door into the passenger seat, and together forever she and the pony-tailed man sped away.

6a. Ambulance

SUSAN HEARD THE ambulance and did what she was supposed to do. That is how she thought of an ambulance: a reason to pull over. She turned her Audi convertible towards a curb of glass and trash. As the tires crunched empty beer bottles and crushed bags filled with who-knows-what, she thought of how strong radial tires were now, how little chance she had of getting a flat.

The ambulance was a Shaeffer van, one of the larger companies in Los Angeles. In fact, a guy she had once known had worked for them as a dispatcher. But that was years ago. The van was red and white and clean, the letters of the company name stenciled carefully in cursive on the sides, just above the phone number. Susan remembered this more than saw it because the ambulance passed by so fast. It sped by her—right in the middle of the road. She felt the wind through the open window of her car.

Stopped at the curb, Susan let her mind drift to other things. She thought of Alan and her leaving him, how he seemed so surprised at first, then so nonchalant.

"I like trashy women," he had said one time. "You should bleach your hair blonde."

"Platinum," he'd said.

She had gone out and done it, then changed it the next day. To coal black.

Susan was startled by the sound of barking dogs. The ambulance had pulled over not far in ahead of her. The driver had opened the back door. Scores of dogs and cats came racing out from inside the vehicle. They filled the sidewalk and the street. There seemed no end to them.

Susan had thought often about ambulances—mostly about their role in traffic, about her automatic response to their sound, about how to distinguish them from police cars and fire trucks, the latter being easy because of the rumble such large engines caused. She had never thought about what they carried, mostly the dead and dying, or those saved from that fate—certainly not about Alan or about dogs and cats.

When the chickens were done coming out of the vehicle, immediately behind the dogs and cats, Susan refastened her seat belt, signaled left, and pulled quickly from the curb, heading straight for the hospital, shouting at the driver of the ambulance as she passed by at a speed well over the posted limit, her own siren blaring.

6b. Homeless Suite—Hollywood

SHE WAS AN older woman, about 60, standing at the end of the Cahuenga offramp. The Hollywood Freeway. Near the Hollywood Bowl. A hot summer night. She was holding a sign: "Fighting Cancer. Need help." Her hands were shaking. She was surrounded by lit candles—candles in long glass cylinders emblazoned with the likenesses of Our Lady of Guadalupe, the Sacred Heart of Jesus, JFK.

I turned on the inside light in my Explorer to look for money in the ashtray. I do not smoke. I rolled down my window—the ac blasting in the August heat—to hand her a dollar. She reached for the money with her left hand. Her nails were long, very long, maybe two inches, and perfectly manicured. She was old, probably dying, and she looked it, but I felt a stirring in my groin at the sight of that beautiful hand. She took the money and I drove off.

She was there again the next morning as I headed for work. I made a special loop around the ramps to help her out again. This time I had a five to give her. She took the money and thanked me, her nails so long, her hands still shaking badly.

7a. Grand Larceny

THE TIRES ON the car were old,
The treads worn thin;
The ignition was easy to pop
With a screwdriver.
The white lines on the road
Were old and faded
Like a dowager's chalky make-up.
The road was wet and slick;
We had been there many times.
With such bald tires,
There was nothing to grip
When Tommy hit the brakes.
The wall came so fast.

7b. Just a Little Bit

THERE IS AN inch or two to take. Not much more. You know the old saying; give him or her an inch, he or she will take a mile. Do we have even that to take? Or to give? I mean, an inch. Really. We must have one somewhere. But, an inch and a mile. That is a major gap. Exaggeration there, I think. A mile is 63360 inches. I know it could be more. The saying could go: give them (I can't worry about gender now) an inch and they'll take ten kilometers—what with the metric system and all. But it doesn't. And we don't; I mean, give them an inch even. So we never find out about the mile, let alone about the foot.

8a. New Shoes

I JUST BOUGHT a new car, and then I bought new shoes. I really liked the shoes. They had thick soles, comfortable and good for wear and tear, but black and white on top, so they were stylish, too.

I knew I would get the girls to like me now.

I couldn't wait to go out to the clubs.

I was bearing right. There was a "YIELD" sign. I saw it and I saw the oncoming cars. But the thick sole of my new shoe caught on the gas pedal and I accidentally accelerated.

The Ryder truck had the right of way, clearly. He ploughed into the driver's side door real good. My car spun around. Shards of steel pierced my side, my leg. Later I remembered that my right shoe came flying off, the groove of the thick sole still stuck under the accelerator.

In the morning when I woke up at the hospital, I noticed my right foot was missing. The nurse informed me that they'd had to amputate. At the ankle. The foot was apparently badly mangled, irreparable.

When they discharged me, the hospital staff gave me back my shoes, both of them. The shoes were in pretty good shape. I shined them up when I got home. Now they are sitting in my closet.

8b. The Tabby Boy

MR. BARRETT COULDN'T see. Even with his glasses. He was the Assistant Principal.

They gathered us at the end of recess so Mr. Barrett could address us. He had an important message.

We had been running around, and sweating. Now we were cold. The fourth and fifth grade classes—nine and ten years old.

"Is the Tabby boy here?" Mr. Barrett asked. "Come up here beside me. The message is for you."

Robert Tabby made his way through the crowd. He was a fat kid who most of us teased.

Mr. Barrett held a slip of paper very close to his eyes—no more than an inch away—and began to read aloud: "Message for Robert Tabby. Your father has died."

You could tell Mr. Barrett was embarrassed, but only after the words had left his mouth. It was clear that he had not read the message himself prior to reading it out loud. Robert Tabby began to cry. Mr. McCarthy led him away to someplace private. The rest of us stood shuffling our feet in the cold, waiting for what came next.

After a full minute of silence, Mr. Barrett cleared his throat, then declared recess over, and ordered us to file back to our classrooms.

Robert Tabby did not come back to school the rest of the week. When he returned, everyone was nice to him—for a week or two.

9a. Don't Walk

WE'D BEEN DRINKING. We were in a hurry. It was the brink of dark. The light was about to change as we whipped around the corner of 2nd Street onto Broadway in downtown Los Angeles. We were headed for Chinatown to meet some girls.

Our light was green. The guy was dressed in dark clothes and he was smack in the middle of the crosswalk. We hit him hard. He bounced off the hood and went over the roof. Even with the radio on loud we could hear him hit the pavement.

Chris was sitting next to me; Chris was freaking out.

He put the gun to his head.

"Chris, don't!"

He pulled the trigger. Pieces of his head splattered on the dashboard, the windows, the windshield.

The cop car was getting closer, the siren louder, the flashing lights brighter.

I had a lot of explaining to do. I was at the wheel.

9b. Accident Part II

IT WAS NOT his car. He was unfamiliar with the controls. He was fiddling around with the instruments protruding from the dashboard and from the steering wheel. He was trying to find the windshield wipers. It was not raining. In fact, it was Los Angeles in July. It has only rained in Los Angles in July twice in the past decade—or so they tell me. Who told me that? I can't remember. In any case, he was attempting to clean the windshield, to improve visibility—dead bugs, smog, grease. It was the middle of the night. There was a great deal of glare. He did not find the wipers. Instead he found the horn. He beeped it accidentally. Not once, but a couple of times. The enraged driver of the car in front of him got out of his car. They were stopped at a red light. The other driver fired two shots, one or both fatal. Our driver did not have a chance to say he was not honking his horn—in fact another's horn—with impatience, but rather merely trying to clean a dirty windshield.

10a. Going Off

Dear Editor:

Regarding your story of March the Fourth re: Colin Ferguson: How do you know what sets a guy off? You don't. There's always all kinds of speculation—he had a bad childhood, he got laid off from the post office, something. But it's all bullshit. It's a funny thing. A guy can be with you all sane and shit and then suddenly, boom!!!, he's got a gun and he's mowing people down. For my two cents' worth, I think it's the little shit—you know, you've had a bad day and some one cuts in front of you at the ATM. It's the straw the breaks the camel's back as they say. You ain't never hurt no one before but all of a sudden you whip out a gun you just so happen to be carrying, and Bang!!!, you shoot his ass. When the reporters come by your neighborhood, all the people on your block say "I don't know how he could have done it. He's always been such a friendly guy, minds his own business, always says hello," you know the routine. But I'm telling you, it can happen to any one. I'm as peaceful as the next guy if you leave me alone, but cross me on a bad day and you never know what you're going to get. I mean, I ain't ever shot no one before, but all's I'm saying is that any one's capable; every one's got their boiling point, their pet peeve, the thing that sets them off. I'll give you a personal example—I hate it when hair keeps popping up in front of my eyes. And I can't brush it away. It happens all the time to me—especially when I'm driving—and it drives me crazy, pardon the pun. I see this strand of hair wiggling in front of my eyes, I try to brush it away, swat at it, the whole nine yards, but it keeps coming back. And I'm about to scream. I solved this one though. It was happening every day for a while and I thought I was going to blow my top right there on the freeway, in my car, but I looked real carefully in the mirror one morning and I found that I had a piece of hair—just one piece—growing out of a mole just under my eye and that piece of hair—when it was struck by the breeze blowing through my car—would just dart up into my field of vision. But I got the sucker; I took a scissors and cut it real close so it can't wave around—and I keep track of it because it grows back. The minute it gets the least bit long, I'm right there with the scissors—little nail scissors do the trick, just the right size. And I'm real glad I got to the bottom of this one, because like I say, you never know what little thing can set a person off.

Yours,

JM
Van Nuys, CA

10b. What Is True?

I NEVER KNOW what's true.

I read the papers, five or six of them. The New York Times, the Washington Post, the Globe, the National Enquirer, the Watchtower, the Los Angeles Sentinel, the Cleveland Plain Dealer.

It's all so confusing.

The OJ trial is a good example. I know it was a decade ago, but what's ten years, really…?

Just an aside: my weight goes up and down. I ate a lot of pasta early on during the Clinton Administration. I thought I was doing the Mediterranean thing. Then I caught on to Atkins. Now I eat bacon and eggs and cheese and red meat. I like Moby and I do feel bad about eating animal flesh, but then I watch the Discovery Channel and I learn about the food chain…well, you know what I mean, so I end up just saying, like, whatever…

And, I kind of like Britney Spears' new album—the songs are sort of catchy and she's way cute (that's not just media hype)—but when I mention this to my friends, they start laughing…I live in Echo Park and most of my friends are a lot cooler than me. They tell me to forget about politics, or they say don't believe what I read, and stuff like that, but I can't do it.

But, anyway, back to the OJ thing—it really still has me going, but in all kinds of directions. I mean, I listen to Matt Drudge or Rush Limbaugh and I feel one way, I mean not about OJ, but about, say, our invasion of Iraq—it seems alright and like it's good to get Saddam, but then I went to this anti-war demonstration in Pershing Square downtown, and I got all caught up in thinking about the innocent victims and our greedy quest for oil and all that kind of shit…oh, fuck, I don't know…

But now, like I said, I've been onto this OJ thing for ten years—I don't have a view one way or the other—I can totally see it both ways—guilty or innocent—I've read all about it, but I've kind of devoted my life, all my spare time at least, to finding the answer.

It's weird what people get into. Like when I went to this opera these people were performing at a dive bar in my neighborhood—it was pretty cool, like it was by Tom Waits or something—and these people outside smoking were all Goth-looking, which makes sense, except this one guy, he had on all purple and gold, a Lakers' jacket and gold Converse and a championship t-shirt from two years ago—so what's up with that?

Anyway, I'm really sleuthing on the OJ thing. Still. It's really important, you know. I've already been banned from going near Nicole's condo. I'd go there, like once a week, on my days off—I work at a Denny's—pretty much at least once a week for the first couple of years, looking for clues, for shit the cops missed. I mean they didn't even clean it up, the courtyard where all the blood was, for the longest time.

As I said, I'm not sure what I believe any more about his guilt or innocence. I was never sure. I mean, back when it happened and during the trial, I'd be sure, but like for a day. Back then I lived down by Washington and Adams, and I'd pick up the Sentinel and they had some good articles. They had this great story about Mark Fuhrman, the main cop, and about his record and right then I thought it was this big conspiracy about race.

But then I read all this other stuff. About how much money he had, and how no regular Joe would ever get off because who can afford Johnnie Cochran? And I never really believed Kato Kaelin anyway. I mean, there's nothing wrong with the guy really, just kind of a slacker, and who am I to talk, but come on, he was just lying because the guy let him stay at his house for free…I'd do that.

And that's like the Clinton thing with Monica, Clinton was kind of like a slacker being President, sitting around the White House, talking on the phone, eating pizza and getting a blow job. I mean, that's cool. It's kind of like me being President, or something. I can relate to that. He's a regular guy. I mean, I go to McDonald's for breakfast, too.

But anyway, OJ put up this reward to find the real killer. That's a motivation, for sure. I'd love to get the reward. I mean, not just for the money—though I won't lie, it's a whole lot of money—but to be the guy that solved the case and all. Man, that would be cool.

I mean, Clinton and OJ. That was the Nineties, right? Like I said, I like Clinton a lot. I think he was a great President. I mean, not just because of the fast food and the blowjobs and stuff. He's really smart. And, I like OJ, too—even though I believe it now—he slashed those fuckers, and they did fuck him over, I mean, like driving his car, a Ferrari, if I remember right, and that waiter guy returning her glasses to her front door—I mean, who does that shit? Really. Like, home delivery of all the shit you left behind. Nobody does that, man, nobody.

Then I made my mistake. I followed OJ down to Florida. Pensacola. Panama City. The whole Panhandle. From one golf course to another. Him, with that girlfriend of his. Paula Something. This hot chick with this stone cold killer. I guess I've made up my mind. I know what I believe now. I mean, I'm in jail and he's not.

11a. Thug Life

I.

IT IS APRIL. It is springtime. I hate this time of the year. There is nothing to anticipate. No Christmas. No New Year's. Even though I hate looking forward to things. They always turn out like shit.

II.

When I went out that night, I was pissed as hell, all upset inside, full of a rage I could not name.

I was going for cigarettes, at maybe three in the morning, walking to the 7-11. It was trash night—all the barrels and the hefty bags out on the street, neatly placed at curbside. When I was through, I'd never seen so much garbage scattered on a single city block.

III.

We had him in the back seat, stretched out on the floor; most of the time he was pretty comfortable; sometimes I'd find myself kicking at him like I was keeping a beat. Then I'd say nice things—things like "it's going to be all right." Then in a minute or two I'd find myself kicking him again, grinding my heels into his face, then it got slippery under the soles of my boots on account of the blood. It was like with a dog, when you kick it, then say "good boy," then kick it again—and you repeat the cycle over and over. (But I think dogs can take it better than humans.)

IV.

I wear gloves on nights like this.

V.

She had a purple mohawk and eleven visible piercings, but they hired her at the Metro Diner anyway. She checked into a cheap motel within walking distance; it was called the Sunshine Inn.

VI.

I never take money for what I do.

VII.

Six months had passed—almost uneventfully, except we still had him with us, drove him around in the car once a day—like taking the dog for a walk—moving from place to place, but all within the city. The Summer was not hot enough for a lot of murder and mayhem on the LA streets, but the Fall came on hard—fires in the hills—Malibu again, and Altadena—followed by floods with the first rains, another part of Malibu, burned away, washed away, cleansed. They're all saying it now: Burn, baby, burn. It's become a cliche.

VIII.

I have trouble with transitions.

We stopped at Bob's, brightly lit on a dark street. She wasn't there. I took care of Bob for Tony and he didn't even ask.

When I got back in the car, I started kicking again.

IX.

She got a job as a dancer.

X.

I crossed the bridge over the LA River at least three times a day. Breakfast, lunch and dinner. Business reasons. I always had him with me, grinding my heels into his face, his chest, his nuts. Every night I went to the club where she worked. I tipped her well, but I never said a word to her. I couldn't. Or couldn't bring myself to; no matter how badly I wanted her.

XI.

I quit my job, but kept my driver. I couldn't let go, couldn't give it up. I got a haircut. I went to the Metro Diner. Of course, she had left that job to go dance at the club. But the Metro had a nice crowd anyhow—a new punk and hip hop group, many colors of hair, piercings, you know, the whole bit. I brought the right books—started with Nietzsche, then Bataille. I figured I could fit in, but I have trouble starting conversations, so I just sat there, drinking coffee and reading my hip books. No one talked to me either. I guess it's the way I look. Some things you can't change. Sometimes I would hear people talking about me. At first it made me feel good; later I got mad.

XII.

I guess I visited the club often enough that she thought of me as a regular. Five nights a week, no fucking surprise. My tips got bigger and bigger. It got so that

when she finished a dance, she would come over and give me a little kiss on the cheek. But I guess since I never spoke, she didn't either. Maybe she was afraid of me, but I don't think so.

She looked less and less uncomfortable up there on stage. I thought I'd like it as she got better. Undulating, so smooth and sensual now. She was so awkward at first. Then she started doing this thing with a live snake. The crowd went wild. I filled up with jealousy. I was surprised at myself; I like slutty women so much.

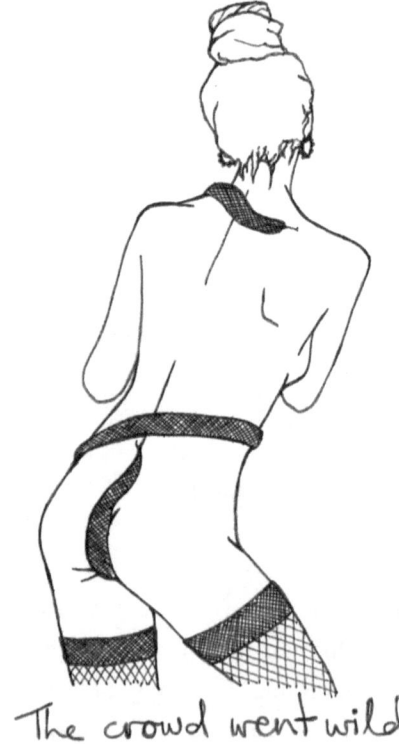

The crowd went wild.
I filled up with jealousy.

XIII.

With no job, I got bored. One day she moved away. I mean, I think so. She just wasn't anywhere any more. No sign of her. Just gone. On the fifth night, I jacked off in the shower thinking about her. Less about her tits, and more about her hair and her hands, which she moved so nicely.

XIV.

By the New Year, he had died. Right there on the floor of the back seat. Only so much one man can take. Surprised he lasted so long. It was beginning to drive me crazy—a lot of work, a lot of upkeep. We just burned the car with the body inside it. It gets real hot in there with the upholstery, the carpets, and all. Hard to identify or trace much of anything. It didn't matter. No one would claim him anyway.

XV.

Like I said, it is April. I have a tee shirt on, but I don't know what it says. I am planning to move across the Los Angeles River for good—where I hope to be just another guy with a gun.

11b. Created Equal?

HOMICIDE VICTIMS, Los Angeles County, June 12, 1994:

* David Abraham, 29 year old male, multiple gunshot wounds

* Ronald Goldman, 25 year old male, multiple stab wounds

* Renee Hurtado, 21 year old female, multiple gunshot wounds

* Alvaro Lopez, 22 year old male, multiple gunshot wounds

* Jaime Moreno, 26 year old male, stab wound to chest

* Nicole Brown Simpson, 35 year old female, multiple stab wounds.

35 year old female
multiple stab wounds.

12a. Bendover #1

SHE DANCED BEHIND the glass.

He was creepier than most—dirty, unkempt, overweight. Not that Matt Damon often stopped by her peep show booth. The only cute guys that ever came in were in college and they usually just giggled, or made fun, and they never spent much money. This guy, she thought, he's a spender.

She had very long legs and very platinum hair, which she bleached over and over, religiously, to way past blonde. She played with her hair for him.

He fumbled with himself and with his money. His hands were grimy.

She started fast. Maybe he'd spend a lot up front and she'd get this over with.

She bent over at the waist and thrust her ass up against the glass. She touched the floor with one long arm, her long silver nails glimmering. She folded her other arm around and past her crotch and fingered herself around her asshole, pulling at the string of her thong.

He seemed to like that. He reached inside his pocket. More money, she hoped. He did pay more, but he also took out a notepad and pen and placed them in his lap.

A reporter? she wondered. For who? For what?

She continued to dance while he scribbled on the paper.

He finished writing and he held the paper up to the glass so she could read it.

"Meet me outside. Five minutes," it said.

She squinted to read the note, and then, disgusted at the thought, she shook her head vigorously.

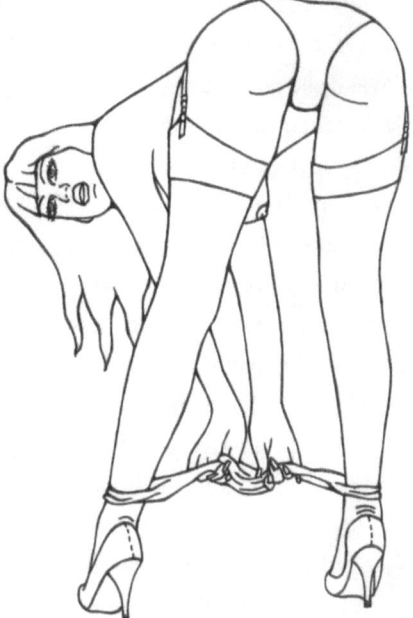

He wrote another note.

"In the alley out back."

He kept paying so she kept dancing. She had sat down and twirled her legs in the air, her spread facing him, but now she got up and looked away.

He wrote another note.

She gave him the finger.

He wrote one more time.

"PLEASE!" he wrote in all capital letters.

All at once, she felt compelled to go outside, to find out what this was all about. She did have a break coming up. She could have a cigarette and find out the story.

She nodded her head yes and finished her dance.

Outside it was breezy and she was cold in her skimpy clothes. She lit a cigarette and waited. He was late in coming out. Chickenshit, she thought. Figures. She did not feel afraid. She'd kicked plenty of ass herself and, besides, her bouncers were just a shout away.

When she'd almost finished her smoke, he lumbered into the alley. The wind was blowing the trash around and a pair of feral cats was climbing in and out of the dumpster.

"What do you want? I haven't got much time," she snarled when he got near.

He came up and stood very close to her.

He did not say a word.

His breath smells good, she thought. He was that close to her.

They stood for a few minutes in silence.

After the bit of quiet went on, she leaned down to kiss him on the forehead. She

was taller than him in her heels. Then she began to unbutton him and she pulled up her skirt. He reached inside his coat, slowly so as not to startle or scare her. To give her money? she wondered. This was her gift. She grabbed his hand, stopped his movement, dug her nails into his palm a little bit, and placed his hand on her tits. She was wet; he was hard. She straddled him against the brick wall and fucked him in silence. No condom. When he'd come inside her, she zipped him back

up and primped herself, smoothing out her skirt, her top, her hair. She turned away from him, then turned back. She kissed him long and hard on the lips, tongued him deeply, then withdrew.

"Bye, sweetie," she said.

She walked as quickly as she could in 5-inch heels back down the alley, towards the street, and the front door of the club. He didn't move at all. Except for her goodbye, neither of them had spoken.

When she reached the street and the light, she greeted Tony, who was working the door, lit another cigarette, took two or three quick puffs, flicked the butt into the gutter and went back to work.

12b. Bendover #2

SHE WAS STANDING at the corner. I approached her.

There was a lot of traffic; it was hard to hear.

"Excuse me?" she said.

I leaned in and whispered close to her ear.

I thought she was going to hit me.

"You're disgusting," she said.

"I'll give you fifty dollars," I said.

"And, you're cheap."

She was dressed in a suit, probably Armani. She was wearing Ferragamo pumps. She had a simple string of pearls around her neck. Her fingernails were very long and unpolished.

"I have a place all lined up," I said.

A police car drove by and slowed down right near us. Neither of us looked at the cops and they took off.

"It's a hotel; it's just down the street," I said.

I thought I was doing too much talking.

"OK," she said.

Once inside the hotel room, she stripped immediately and without fanfare, and told me to do the same, which I did.

"Bend over," she said.

I bent over and waited for what came next.

13a. Ms. Ethereal

She was standing by the bar, all in red and black.
I ordered another drink.
It was just after midnight.
I called her "Miss Ethereal."
She didn't know what I was talking about.

13b. Roommates

SHE MOVED IN as a roommate. She was menacing. All tattoos, and black leather and chains. I fell in love with her right away. She parked her motorcycle inside the apartment. She loved birds. She would sneak up to the roof of our place, four floors above Hollywood Boulevard, to feed the pigeons and the sparrows, the occasional seagull, and the crows. Her friends started to come around. I tried to drink with them. Sometimes I had dope for them. Then they came to expect it. One night, they began to hit me. In my own apartment. First with their fists, then with clubs and chains. She did nothing to stop them. I think she may have even struck a few blows herself. Someone called an ambulance. The EMTs took me to the hospital and she stayed home drinking with the guys who beat me. They broke my nose and some of my ribs. The doctor told me I was lucky it was not worse. I came home the next morning. Her friends were still there. One chick handed me a beer. "No hard feelings," another guy said. My roommate laughed and we all drank together. When she decided to move to Seattle, of course I went with her.

14a. East Hell

PHOENIX SCARES THE hell out of me.

Like nowhere else.

I met her in LA. At the airport. LAX. She was going to Phoenix. Unclear why. I'd never been there. We were tonguing each other while she was waiting for her flight. She asked me to accompany her. That's how she put it. I had no plans, nowhere to go. I went along. She said her name was Vonda.

We took a cab out of Sky Harbor, the Barry Goldwater Terminal.

"To the nearest hotel," she said.

We drove west on Washington: a wasteland of scrap metal yards and rental car storage lots. Barren; bleak. Both words insufficient.

We found a place. The Desert Star. Unaffiliated with a chain, I assumed. A bed, a TV we never turned on; two bars of soap. No shampoo. No conditioner. No lotion. The sound of junkyard dogs guarding the cars parked next door. Vipers, Lamborghini's, Ferrari's: Resort Car Rentals. On the other side, a crushing operation: scrap metal, export. Trucked to the nearest harbor—likely, Long Beach or San Pedro.

I closed my eyes.

I wanted her so bad.

They say guys fall asleep right after sex. I never do—she slept soundly and I left her there to get a good night's rest. I'd paid for the room, such as it was, in advance.

It was four in the morning when I left. My billfold was empty. I'd paid cash at the hotel and that cleaned me out. I'd wanted anonymity. I still had a plane ticket. There was a flight at six. I decided to walk to the airport.

Within a block, I got jumped. Marauders. They just wanted money. Problem was I didn't have shit. They beat the fuck out of me because I was broke. I thought of hopping the fence to escape, but the dogs guarding the cars were on the other side. I figured I was better off with the muggers; I think I made the right decision. The dogs would have torn my ass up.

It was a long walk but I made my early morning flight. Back to LA, back to Paradise, you know.

Like I said, Phoenix scares the hell out of me.

14b. The Big Island

CORA KEPT A nice bar, clean and neat, and I stopped in every night. She was a skinny girl with legs like stir sticks. When she announced to the world that she was pregnant, she immediately pronounced me as the father, though I'd never seen her anywhere except behind the bar.

Despite the impossibility of my paternity, I proclaimed fatherhood. (I became Cora's champion.) I don't know why. I guess I thought I'd never have another chance.

Oh, Cora.

* * *

Over the next few weeks, I didn't spend much time with her.

A few months after the baby was born, someone busted into Cora's apartment. I wasn't there. Neither was the kid, who was spending the night at her grandmother's. Cora was there—unfortunately. The home invasion robbers busted up Cora's apartment and they busted up Cora.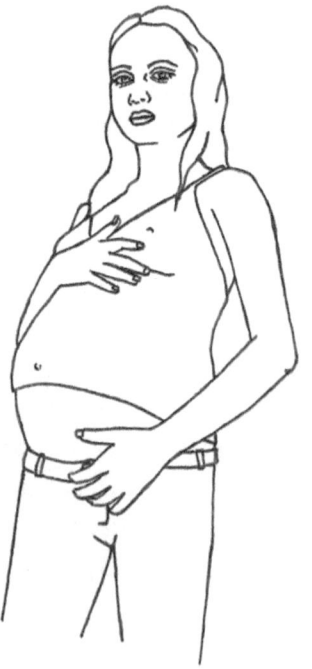

She said they didn't rape her—who knows—but somehow they cracked a number of her vertebrae. She ended up in a wheelchair.

I took on increased responsibility for the baby. We named her Danielle—after no one we knew of.

A year or so later, Cora died of complications from her spinal cord injuries.

During the three plus weeks it took her to die— something inside her crushing something else inside her—I never left her side.

The guys who beat her were convicted of assault and battery and they each got eight years. Now that Cora's dead, the DA says he'll file murder charges. I'm for that.

Danielle is seven now. She was really cute in the school Christmas pageant. She was an angel in the afternoon show, a snowflake in the evening.

These days I stay home a lot. I never go to bars.

I think Danielle should have a brother or a sister, but although I never dated Cora, I can't seem to bring myself to date anyone else either. I feel I'm still in mourning.

Oh, Cora.

15a. Baby

WE WERE AT a bar in Chinatown, but there were no Asian people there. Joan and I were sitting in a far corner, trying to be alone. But it was crowded.

"Excuse me," I said. "Excuse me."

I was heading for the bathroom. They wouldn't move.

"Ah, that's short for 'get the fuck out of the way,'" I said.

I pushed the big guy. He did nothing.

Joan and I had been fighting.

When I got back from the men's room, the guys were gone.

So was she.

* * *

She had the baby, but it was hard for her. He placenta broke up during delivery and she bled a lot.

The kid was fine, but they stuck the hell out of Joan with IVs. She lost a great deal of blood. The kid was swaddled in the nursery—of course, unaware.

* * *

I sent her a present and one for the baby. They were nice gifts.

* * *

She sent me a thank you note and time went by. Without much money, she cooked Kraft macaroni & cheese and top ramen for herself. She was still nursing.

A thousand miles away, I made frozen pizza (Celeste is still my favorite kind) and drank cheap vodka.

* * *

A year later, I called her up. I hadn't called before.

"He's not yours," she said.

"I know," I said.

We talked for another minute or so. That was it.

15b. Doorstep

SHE SAT ON broken concrete stairs amidst shards of shattered glass. She wore open-toed, five-inch high heels in red patent leather. Her feet were dirty, but not filthy. She picked her inch-long ragged toenails, splattered with purple and other colors of polish, with her jagged and varied fingernails. Let's take the fingernails one at a time:

- the left thumbnail: 4 inches long, unpainted
- left index finger: bitten well beyond the quick, to the point of bleeding, splotches of red polish
- left middle finger: half-an-inch long, broken at an angle, clear polish
- left ring finger: 7 inches long, shaped like a curly fry, half-painted
- left pinkie: bitten way back, painted green
- right thumbnail: bitten, dirty like an auto mechanic's
- right index finger: 5 inches long, immaculate and painted intricately in a Byzantine design
- right middle finger: missing
- right ring finger: 1/2 inch, "classy" French manicure
- right pinkie: 9 inches long, splotchy blue polish

K-Mart's has closed 17 stores. Lay-offs are imminent, up to 400 workers.

War is raging. Spoiled food is causing salmonella outbreaks.

Some guys can't stop coming back. The variety is just too much. More complex than Wittgenstein, certainly. The questions: ontological, not epistemological.

Let's describe the toenails:
- all approximately the same length, but rough, unfiled, almost serrated at the tips,
- jagged, seemingly uncared for, yet special.

She has secret names for each one. They are truly secret, clandestine, private. I don't know them. Honest.

The whole world is clearly described in the nineteen appendages: the theory of everything (TOE), Genesis, a new cosmology …

Just one story: John met her on the street, on the very steps, in fact. Worth maybe $10 million. He'd sold his company that made electronic orange peelers pitched on late night TV. The successor to RONCO, a worthy forebear no doubt. This time more contemporary, available on the Net, its own Web Site, etc., the whole nine yards.

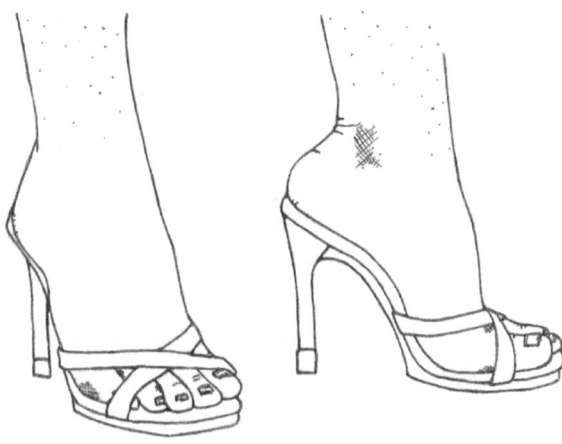

An American story: made it, then lost it all in six months. They spent it together. The high life, for sure, but other things, too. Her nails became their crystal ball, their map of the world. But the clairvoyance eluded them. They bled cash.

Funny thing: her nails—fingers and toes—really are the map of the world. Difficult as shit to read, however. You know, the many incomprehensible products of expertise and shit. Now, after all, on the doorstep: new and continued fascination—of a different kind to be sure—but a life still with each other. All else intolerable.

16a. Antojitos

THERE'S NOTHING IN the mailbox. Not even junk mail.

I wanted her to grow her fingernails. She said she'd think about it. She forgets to cut her toenails though. I love that.

I'm glad McDonald's has dollar specials now. I like the Big N' Tasty. It's the only item at Mickey D's that has regular mayonnaise, no special sauce. I hate special sauce.

We cannot represent simultaneity in literature or in film, no matter how hard we try. "Meanwhile, back at the ranch" does not work. Split screens do not cut it. I'd rather the "meanwhile," in fact. But, you've got to admit it, "Rashomon" is somewhere in the neighborhood.

Significance is difficult. If a stray dog walks up and stops nearby—say, the same picture frame—while I wait for a bus: is it a symbol of something? Is it random? Is it meaningless? Does the dog live or die? Do we care?

She started biting her fingernails. Oh, well. She asked me not to take it personally. She said she was under a lot of stress at work.

I cut flowers from my neighbor's yard –without permission—and put them in a vase on the kitchen table. They droop almost immediately. She feigns not to notice.

I do not like exterminators. William Burroughs is the exception. I like him, but he is dead now. When we have infestations at the house—no matter what kind: termites, ants, rodents—I fight like hell against calling the pest control company.

I like trains and train stations. They contradict themselves so well. I love both the college couple cuddling in the corner, one of them about to depart, and the man with the shopping cart, slouched and sleeping on one of the waiting room benches. It is so different from an airport, or a dentist's office, for that matter.

I grow to love her chewed up fingers. I start to suck her fingertips and nibble around her cuticles. She purrs when I do it.

Her toenails are still long. I don't say a word, but I suck on her toes, too. She seems to like it.

I have six messages on my answering machine. Each one is full of silence, no words uttered. The beep, the quiet hiss, the click of their hanging up. That's it. Not even the smooth modulation—or the nervous hesitancy, depending on experience—of a telemarketer's voice.

* * *

Morning noon and night. I miss the distinctions.

I am lonely and alone. We have grown apart.

I want to have another drink, only without your patronizing me, or sympathizing with me, or pitying me, or judging me, or recommending a self-help group.

Fuck you, in fact. You go to hell.

Antojitos are the most elegant food. You don't need utensils. Everything is rolled up and you can eat it all with your fingers. I love it so much. I only eat in Mexican restaurants. I love to watch you eat with your bitten fingernails.

We are all gone from one another. Yearning is a natural condition.

I go to the King Eddie Saloon on Skid Row to pick up women. Most of them are homeless. I don't mind. I don't mind at all.

16b. Chalk line

1. WE SHOOT OUT the streetlights and tear down the street signs. We don't like strangers.

2. He went into the bar; he never came out. We got the money.

3. We like to watch ourselves on TV.

4. The space we work in is narrow. The scant light creates long shadows like toothpicks. We all wear the same thing. We never had day jobs to quit.

5. The take is down. We realize we must tinker with the environment. We hope and pray the changes aren't major.

6. "Hey, I said `don't be messing with your hair.'"

17a. Casper

HE COULD NOT hear because he was deaf and so therefore he did not hear either the gunshots or the police sirens. He was not hit by a bullet, but he was arrested.

He met her in a bar.

She looked exactly like the Black Dahlia.

His previous girlfriend wore a mullet. He picked her because of, not despite, her haircut.

The Black Dahlia's hair was big—Jackie Kennedy, pre-Jackie-O.

He got off the bus at a stop, in a city, that he did not know.

He did it on purpose.

He was detained actually and not arrested. He did not know the identity of the dead man.

* * *

He got a job at a firing range, which was ideal because he couldn't hear.

The owner said he was going to argue for a waiver of workers' compensation insurance because there was no chance of injury—at least to his ears.

The police screened him before he was hired. His arrest at the shoot-out came up but he was cleared because he was never charged with a crime.

* * *

At the dark bars on Cahuenga, he could not see the Black Dahlia in the un-light, but she was there.

At Sparkling Laundroland he asked her name.

"Elizabeth," she said.

Creeped out, he walked away without another word.

Did she know? he wondered.

He was sure he'd read her lips correctly.

For the record, she thought he looked cute in his David Bowie-in-his-Ziggie Stardust-days-sort-of look.

* * *

Pigeons flew in and out of the abandoned warehouse.

* * *

About a week later, he follows the Black Dahlia into the Laemmele on Sunset where she is attending a movie alone.

In the dark and anonymously, not to mention uncharacteristically, he grabs her ass as she walks down the aisle. She jumps, startled, but she does not know who it is. He is quick to move away. So as not to attract notice, he stays for the whole film though he cannot hear it.

On the way out, in silence, he takes her by the hand. They go to a bar in Koreatown, but there are no Koreans there. Everybody is either real tall or real short. He and the Dahlia are the only normal-sized people there, though she is borderline, about 5'4." The walls of the bar are painted bright red and bright yellow and the track lights are aimed straight at the colorful walls, but neither up nor down, giving the place a kind of intentional sideways feel. Everyone's drink is bright green. The music is Norteno though the clientele is not Latino. He sits down with the Black Dahlia in a far booth, black Naugahyde, and they make out for two hours without exchanging a word. At midnight, he finds her a cab.

17b. Ricky and Sharon

THE AIR OF the night clung to the skin like a spider's web. The streetlights stood up from the sidewalk like scepters held by illuminated hands. The corner mailbox was tipped on its side and covered with black spray paint. The wind was full of the smell of garbage and burnt grease. Cats' claws had pierced bags of trash left at the curb and the scattered contents lined the gutter with paper and chicken bones, cans and cigarette butts.

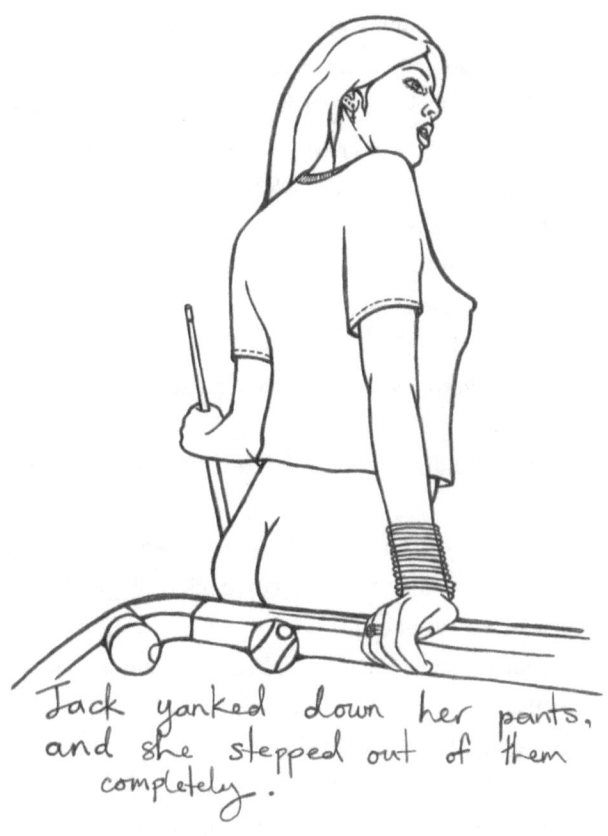

Jack yanked down her pants, and she stepped out of them completely.

The motorcycles were lined up outside 'Katie's.' The bar was at the end of a dark and dead-end street, nestled among closed factories and shuttered shops. All the buildings were splattered with graffiti; the pavement was covered with broken glass. Inside, people were playing pool and watching the news. Poz and Paul and Ricky were clutching at Sharon.

"You know, they had this thing on the National Geographic about polar bears," Jack said. "Doris and I watched it last night."

"How was it?" Ricky asked. He grabbed Sharon's ass. She slapped him hard in the face. He laughed. "Did you see that?" he said.

"They're incredible," Jack kept on. "When they bed down for the winter, they build igloos. Then they keep them exactly thirty-five degrees. If it gets colder, they wake up and rebuild it."

"Sharon, will you fuck me?" Ricky asked. She poured her drink on him. Sharon had broken up with Ricky six months ago.

Two other women put money in the jukebox. When Sharon came back from the bathroom, Paul called her over and said:

"Sharon, Jack, listen: I have a proposition for you. I'll give both $20 if you let Jack eat you out on the pool table right here. What do you say?"

"I'm a married man," Jack said.

The other guys laughed.

"Jack won't do it. She's not a fucking polar bear," Ricky said.

They laughed again.

"Put up the money," Jack said.

"Hey Sharon, what about you?" Paul asked. "You haven't said nothing. Jack can't eat himself."

"Two hundred bucks," she said. "If you ain't got it, go get the rest of the guys to pony up."

Sharon played a game of pool while Paul made the rounds, collecting money.

"I've got a hundred and sixty bucks," Paul said. He showed the money to Sharon. She snatched it out of his hand.

Sharon stepped out of her heels and unbuttoned her jeans. Her feet were pale, her toenails red.

"You pull them down, Jack."

Jack yanked down her pants, and she stepped out of them completely. She rubbed her hand along her crotch and turned to show her bare ass to the guys. They whistled and hollered.

"Let me see your tongue," she said to Jack.

He stuck it out complacently.

"Nice and long," she said.

The shouting continued. Ricky bought everyone a drink. Poz' breathing was heavy and jerky.

Sharon climbed up onto the pool table, tucked her toes in the pockets, and spread her legs, her knees in the air. Jack crouched down at the narrow end of the table, put his chin on the felt, and began to lick. She ran her nails through his hair and along his neck. Ricky and Paul and the guys crowded around pushing each other. Poz watched the action on the pool table intently and silently. Sharon had the $160 clutched tight in her left hand.

"Harder, Jack," she said. "Lick me hard. Suck it; bite me. Come on."

Ricky said, "Hey, Sharon, I'll give you another twenty if you give me a turn."

"Fuck you," she said. She started moaning and pulling Jack's hair, pushing his head firmer against her crotch.

"Hey look," Paul said. "She's coming."

Ricky pushed through the other guys and shoved Jack out of the way. He crouched and stuck out his tongue. Sharon stood up on the table and kicked his face with her bare foot.

"Jack, yes; but not you, asshole," she said.

Jack scrambled to his feet. He punched Ricky and the place went up, every one swinging bottles and pool sticks and wrestling into the video games.

Ricky was on the ground, and Sharon, still naked from the waist down, bent over and scratched his face hard with her long nails.

He screamed, "I'm going to get you, bitch."

Jack had him pinned to the ground and kept pummeling him.

Sharon slipped on her pants, then her shoes. She ground a spike heel into Ricky's face before she walked out the door.

"Goodbye, Ricky sweetheart," she said.

Poz was pissed. He wanted to go next with Sharon. He'd wanted to fuck her—fuck anyone—for such a long time.

18a. Risky Behavior

GAIL AND TOM had fought. When they'd finished arguing, she insisted on walking the dog at midnight, clearly a risky venture. Tom argued against it—vociferously.

"I hate when you do this," he yelled. "Is this your way of punishing me? Put yourself in danger!? Worry the shit out of me?!"

She went to get the leash and said nothing.

He continued shouting:

"You're just fucking with me, Gail!"

"It's not safe!"

"This is LA; not Bangor, Maine!"

Gail ignored him, went out anyway, angry, slamming the door behind her. She walked quickly and for a long time.

Tom turned on the television. The late night shows were boring. He fell asleep in front of Conan O'Brien.

She walked the long way in order to cool off. It was a cool, clear night. Jason the dog was being good. Her spirits were beginning to lift. By the time it struck her that Tom really would be worried, she was more than 15 minutes away, even at a brisk pace.

Gail turned around immediately and began almost to jog. She was breathing hard as she came up the stairs to the front door. Jason started to bark. While she fumbled for her keys, Jason pushed the door open with his snout. In anger, she had forgotten to lock the door on her way out. That was their deal: the last one out was responsible for locking the door behind them. There was a silver lining though, she thought. She felt she could apologize for that, maybe start the process of making up.

But, the place was a mess, things scattered all over the floor, a total disaster. She didn't see her husband anywhere.

"Tommy, what the fuck did you do this time?" she screamed.

He'd broken stuff in anger before, but never like this, and it was so very long ago. Now, the living room was trashed, completely fucked up. Gail began to cry.

The signs that something more was wrong came to her only gradually. As she scanned the room, she noticed the television, the stereo system, a silver statuette, all were missing. The lamps and their glass collectibles were broken, and there was blood on the floor, more blood than would come from a cut made by a shard of glass. In fact, a trail of blood, in heavy pools, led through the living room and the den towards the kitchen and the wall phone there.

Gail shrieked before she saw the body. Tom was on the floor, in the kitchen, cut up, covered in blood, phone in hand, clearly dead. Gail stood frozen. The police arrived within five minutes. It was a nice neighborhood in West Los Angeles; they got good response time from the LAPD. Tom must have gotten through on 911 because she had done nothing.

When she saw the cops, Gail shouted: "I didn't do it!"

"Relax, ma'am," the Sergeant said. "We know you didn't do it. Your neighbor saw you out there with the dog and she saw some men drive away from your house. It was a home invasion robbery. That's the name for it now. It's become increasingly common."

The Sergeant paused. "Sorry about your husband," he finally uttered.

Gail was up all night. The coroner came for Tom's body. They would hold it for forensic investigation, conduct an autopsy. Detectives would look for clues. Police came to the house to dust for fingerprints and gather evidence. Neighbors, frightened themselves, came over to comfort Gail. They brought food, even though it was the middle of the night. They urged her to stay with them, with her mother, at a hotel. Gail refused. She wanted to be alone, she told them. She wanted to be at home. It got to be five AM. Finally, everyone was gone.

Before going upstairs to bed, Gail checked the front door—once, twice, three times, maybe more—to make sure it was unlocked.

18b. I'm Fine: The Clinton Years

WE LIVE NEAR Vermont, the new "it" street in LA; Vermont has replaced Melrose, which is all tourists now. We have lived here a long time.

My wife and I park behind the Christian Science Church that used to be a bank. The Funny Farm Tattoo parlor is still open. I had all my tattoos done before they had a place in the neighborhood, but people say the Funny Farm does good work. Vanda says, "I may give them a try. I want something on my calf." I am surprised because she has four tattoos and has been saying four is enough. I want her to get more so I shut my mouth so as not to say anything to discourage her.

On the way to the movies we stop at the Onyx for a cup of coffee. It is May, but it rained like hell earlier in the day so it's barely touching 50 degrees out. There is still a fine mist in the sharp air. "It's not raining hard enough to bother with the umbrella," Vanda says. I am still quiet. At the outside tables you can smell clove cigarettes. We go inside.

The Onyx has art shows. There are altered Barbie dolls all over the place—voodoo Barbie, vampire Barbie, Barbie in a coffin. Alisa is working the counter. She has 31 piercings. I got up the nerve to ask her once. "Just like Baskin Robbins," she said.

On our way out, a homeless man is standing without shoes or coat in the cold. He has a thin blue blanket wrapped tightly around himself. He stands under the awning of a closed thrift shop to avoid the drizzle.

He says "hello" and Vanda and I both talk to him. We stop to chat; we have two to three minutes of conversation, maybe more, albeit mostly about the weather. For whatever reason,. We tell him we're going to see "The Spanish Prisoner." He nods. We say goodbye.

"He must be freezing his ass off," my wife says.

"Fucking welfare reform," I say.

Phil Ochs had it right. I hate liberals. All they do is talk. Our generation: we may be washed up now, but we did it in the sixties. At least we went out into the streets. I think all these thoughts as Vanda and I walk, in silence now. We know nothing of irony.

I stop to look in the bookstore window. The flyer taped to the door says there is a reading next Friday night about "Modern Primitives."

"Look," I say.

"Come on," Vanda says. "We're going to be late for the movie."

By complete coincidence, our neighbors Andy and Sindy are in line at the Los Feliz 3. Andy writes for the LA Weekly; we tell him about the homeless guy by the Onyx.

"Maybe we should all adopt a homeless person," Sindy says.

After the movie, we stand around and talk with Andy and Sindy for a while. We analyze the film. I do not really want to invite our neighbors for drinks. I want to take Vanda to the Dresden—alone.

It is still misting.

"I'm getting cold," Vanda says.

"We got to go," I say.

"Let's have dinner some time," Sindy says.

"We're parked at the post office," Andy says, pointing north and west.

"We're down here," I say, pointing south.

We say goodbye to our neighbors. We will never have dinner with them.

Outside the Onyx, the man is still there. My wife is shivering. She looks at me. I fish around in my pockets. I find a dollar. It is the least I can do.

I hold out the dollar.

"You need some help?" I ask.

"No," he says. He is smiling. He is friendly, but firm. He looks me in the eye.

I extend my hand further.

"Go ahead; take it," I say.

"I'm fine," he says—curtly this time, I think.

I stand there for a few minutes, looking stupid. I don't think he can see me as well as I can see him. Thank God.

I withdraw my hand in silence. I don't know the expression on my face. I know his; I remember it.

I fold the dollar in my hand, ready to stuff it back in my pocket.

Vanda is looking at me. She has been the whole time. Looking at me, that is; not at the homeless man. Before I get the money back in my pants, Vanda grabs it from my hand. She thrusts it towards the homeless man. He does not reach for it. In the rain and the light of the street lamp, I watch the dollar bill flutter to the ground. None of the three of us reaches down to pick it up. I hear Vanda sigh. The homeless man has been breathing deeply the whole time. I am unaware of any sound that I am making.

Vanda spins on her heels and begins walking briskly to the Christian Science Church parking lot where we have our car. Five dollars for the whole night. A good deal, but the church must make some serious money because the lot is always full. I look from the homeless man to Vanda. Her ass is swaying nicely in her tight black jeans. But she is walking ahead of me, faster than me, in single file. I follow her towards the car. I look over my shoulder like Orpheus. The man does not turn into a pillar of salt. I cannot mention drinks or the Dresden or Marty and Elayne to Vanda. She is walking really fast. She waits for me at the car, but the night—and maybe more—is all over. That much is certain.

29a. Scarlett Jo

THE BAND IS playing. They are sitting at the bar. They are facing each other; they are not facing the band. There is love between them, just not that kind of love.

The band is loud and they cannot hear each other, but it doesn't matter.

Time passes.

They have another drink and then another.

They chose this place to meet.

She is blonde; he has dark hair.

The band plays an encore.

They both want to be painters and they have been talking about art: Jean Dubuffet and Basquiat, and the John Currin retrospective at the Whitney, and the upcoming Biennial.

It seems they talked about all this, but truly they cannot hear one another. So it is hard to say.

They are ready for another round.

They kiss between songs and during songs.

The place is lit like Ziggy Stardust, even though the music is retro British punk. Perhaps they should have been at a jazz club, but it doesn't matter.

They miss last call and the lights come on.

The bartender gives them each another drink.

He walks her to her car.

19b. 86ed

IT'S THIS FUCKED up bar scene. She's way cute—she doesn't even see me. She's bartending and the bar is busy.

This guy walks in. He's smoking a cigar. It's New Orleans. Right off I know he's an asshole. He confirms it. He snaps his finger at the bartender—to get her attention.

I react right away. I hit the guy—hard.

The fight spills out onto Bourbon Street. He's bleeding. There are no cops in sight. The bouncer separates us, and the asshole guy starts to walk away. Then he starts saying some shit to me, over his shoulder. I shout back and take a step towards him. His friends push him down the street—away from me. I'm still hopping mad.

When I try to go back inside, the bouncer turns me away. I'm 86 ed, I can't believe it. She'll think I'm just another asshole, the bartender will. She'll never know why I did what I did—for her.

20a. The Red Lion Tavern

THE LEVEL OF conversation sucks. I don't know what the fuck people are talking about—their dogs, their hair, some other bullshit. I see this chick I have a crush on. I think she hates me. I'm married and she knows it and I think she thinks I'm a scumbag, but tonight I had a fight with my wife, so what the fuck...

A whole fucking gaggle of people at the end of the bar order jagermeisters, which I hate, but—again—what the fuck. I buy them all a round. Then they want to talk to me, but I don't want to talk to them, so I'm stuck. I'm now in the middle of these eight people drinking shots and I can't even see chickie who I like. I mean, maybe she's even hanging out upstairs—there's a bar up there, too. So it's like I've got to attract attention, and I'm not sure how. I want her to see me, to notice me, to pay me some attention. I drink the shot of jagermeister, and it tastes like cough medicine. So I buy everybody another round. This one guy keeps calling me "dude." He's nice enough, but it gets to bothering me. I still can't see my girl.

The bathrooms are upstairs, so maybe if I go upstairs to take a piss I'll run into her up there. How lame though. It feels like I'd be chasing her, and that wouldn't look right. And, what would I say, "Oh, I had to go to the bathroom?" So I stay downstairs, and the waitress keeps telling me I should buy a hand-painted beer stein for a hundred bucks. I think, shit, my girl might like that as a gift. But I don't even know where she's hanging out right now, so I buy one of the expensive mugs for the waitress. I mean, it's just random, but my credit card's up to like 200 bucks now.

So I figure if I want my girl, I better do something a little more effective. Sooner than later. Like now. So this guy—my buddy now that I'd bought him two drinks—keeps calling me dude. I'm really annoyed. In fact, I hate his ass. So it comes to me. I have a good-sized knife stuffed down my pants. I kind of keep it there. At all times. So I wait until he calls me dude again—it's kind of an excuse—and I shank him good. The blood gathers; the crowd gathers. She comes downstairs. With everybody else. To see what the commotion is all about. She's a face in the crowd, but she has that look. The cops arrive. They take me away in handcuffs, of course. I don't deny anything. The evidence is clear, the witnesses. I did it out in the open. Obviously. I wanted her to notice.

I can see her wave at me when the police lead me away.

20b. Not a Rat

HE HAD A gun, and he showed me his gun, but he did not point it at me.

He told me he was going to rob Al's store.

I hated Al. He ripped us all off. Seven bucks for a pack of cigarettes. When everybody else was five. Three bucks for a gallon milk. You got to be shitting me!

"You'll get caught."

"I need the money."

He paused.

"I should shoot you," he continued.

"Why?"

"Because you know."

"Aw, I'm not going to tell anyone."

"You sure?" he asked, wrinkling his nose this time.

"Of course not," I said reassuringly, though I didn't know what 'not' meant in this context.

He thought for a while, and then, without another word, he stormed out of my shop.

I did nothing. I called no one—not the cops, not my girlfriend, not anybody.

The next day in the paper, I read he was in jail.

I knew he'd think I had something to do with it. Fuck me, I said aloud.

I called Tina, my girlfriend, and I told her what happened and I laughed.

She thought I was being weird.

Afterwards, I checked at the police station every day to see when he would get out of jail.

21a. Telefono

I WALKED INTO the phone booth speaking only English; I came out speaking Spanish, too.

There were a hundred or so people in the booth when I first went in. At first I didn't like it, but there were enough phones and I got used to it.

It was a rainy day and every one needed a phone. The phone booth was as large as a new car showroom, but still it was crowded. I took one of only two available phones. The phones were hung on the wall only six inches apart. Privacy was difficult, but mine was not a private conservation. I could hear if I covered my left ear. I have large ears and, in high school, the kids used to tease me. Now I wear my hair long to cover my ears. In high school my parents made me cut my hair. I swept my hair back to insert my finger deep in my ear. When I did that I could hear just fine. My hearing is good. That helped me and hurt me in this case. While I could hear the dispatcher on the other end of the phone—I needed a cab—it was hard to block out the surrounding noise. Still I could hear just fine. Later, when I got home, I told my wife I could hear just fine. Of course, I told her in Spanish, which she did not understand and she was puzzled.

"What are you saying, honey?" she asked. Later. That was much later. When I got home.

21b. Mishap at the Gas Pump

IT WAS MID-JULY; it was 90 degrees; it was a mess, and people started acting crazy. It was like everybody forgot how to drive at the same time. Cars pulled up to the gas pumps from all directions and at all angles. It got so you couldn't get in or out. You'd finish pumping your gas and you were stuck. Horns blared. Tempers flared. I had to play cop: direct traffic, settle disputes, prevent violence.

I was losing track of my customers. The guy in the Buick—did I check his oil or not? The lady in the Jeep—did I wash her windows? The riot grrrl at Self-Serve sure had a nice ass. Then I got tied up negotiating with some snob in a Boxster. He wouldn't back up to let a woman in a Volvo station wagon get out. She had three wailing kids in car seats, and she was screaming at the asshole, but he wouldn't budge. I yelled at him, too. He threatened to tell the owner. I told him to fuck off, but handed him a twenty-dollar UNOCAL gift certificate and he sped off without a word, the cheap fuck. Clearly, I was getting pretty upset, but I thought I still had my wits about me. I was wrong.

It was on the news. I remembered the car—a purple vintage Chevy Malibu. The guy was really nice, too. Amidst the chaos, he told me to hang in there. I thanked him and ran off to tell some guy in a pick-up to turn his stereo down; I couldn't think. It was confusing enough. He was cool about it. When I turned around the guy in the Malibu was gone. I 'd checked his fluids. I wasn't sure if I had finished. But I must have...he had driven off. Channel 13 reported that a young actor—I didn't catch the name, but I had thought he looked familiar—was driving west on the 10 when his hood flew open. He had tried to move from the left lane towards the shoulder, but with zero visibility, he slammed into a concrete overpass. Dead on impact.

22a. Removing the Body

THE BODY IS there, on the pavement, in public view.

I make up a story about his death. It is lurid—of course.

In the first version, it is a stabbing. Option number two: he is shot. Then, an accidental death of some kind. A valiant but failed rescue attempt. I know his story, his biography. I am certain. The cops are there—in force. They do not know. I accumulate details. I've got it now.

He is anonymous: 'John Doe,' the police say. They tell me to leave. I fight back. I want to go home, I say, though it is not true. The police are blocking my way. I argue that I should be able to pass through. I lose. They are conducting an investigation, they say. Possible homicide. They are turning away everybody, not just me, they tell me. This much is true. There are police barricades. The street is completely blocked off. I give up. I do not tell them what I know. I don't see shit. I leave without further ado. I go to the nearest bar. I get drunk. I linger there. I watch television. It is official. There is no murder, no death, no killing, no dying. None at all.

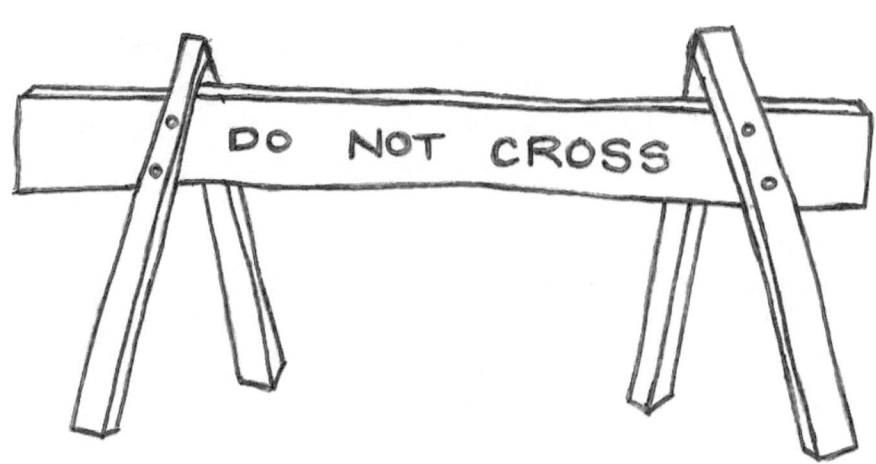

22b. Groceries

I HAD WALKED up four flights of stairs, two bags of groceries in my arms. I guess he was waiting on the landing. I fumbled with my keys, and–off balance–I unlocked my door. He pushed me inside. I fell and the groceries scattered along my small interior hallway. Glass broke and cans rolled. He locked the door behind us.

I tried to get up but he pushed me back down, face first onto the linoleum floor. I am pretty strong but he was stronger. He tied my hands behind my back and pulled down my pants. He asked me not to yell or scream, and for some reason, I complied. He was hard right off. I could feel his cock stiff against my ass cheeks as he hunted around to push it in. I couldn't see him very well; if I turned my head, he'd slap me. I stared at the bevy of groceries littered on my floor. An orange had rolled to rest right near my face. He fucked me hard. I winced at first, and then relaxed. He took about ten minutes to shoot his cum inside me.

There was no after-sex cigarette. He zipped up, half-untied me so I'd still have a little work to do to get loose, then ran out the door.

A neighbor had heard all the noise. She was standing outside my door when he opened it. He pushed her out of the way and barreled down the stairs.

She came to comfort me. She was old and from Russia.

"You poor thing," she kept saying to me.

A police car had apparently been quite close. They caught him just outside the building's front door.

My girlfriend met me at the police station. After much wrangling, I declined to press charges. She was quite upset with me. I told her I wanted to be alone. I went home by myself. I picked up the intact groceries and put them away and swept up the broken glass.

Two nights later I found him sitting at the bar around the corner.

I asked him about the attack.

He told me he'd seen me around the neighborhood, had become obsessed with me, wanted to know me, to fuck me. He said he had stalked me for a week or so. Maybe a little longer. When he saw me walk to the store that day, he went to my apartment building and waited for me to come back. He was going to talk to me, but he couldn't bring himself to. He knew I wouldn't understand. He brought rope just in case...

I bought him a drink. We drank quickly. He bought the next round. And so on. I took his hand, caressed it. That night we went to his house.

PART III

WORKING CLASS HEROES.

"A working class hero is something to be…"
John Lennon, "Working Class Hero" (1970)

Not Working

HE THOUGHT IT was a good idea to take the kids to the movies, and so he did, but when he got there, he had no money, so he snuck them in, the father, too; and the usher saw them, he thought, but didn't say anything—everybody knew about the layoffs. Martha thought the movies were too violent and a waste of money, so she didn't come, and in fact, didn't like him to take the boys; thought they were too young, but he liked Clint Eastwood, and so did they, so they saw a "Dirty Harry" picture. It was a new release. They got to cheer together awhile when Harry shot the villain, so they felt better for a short time. On the way home, still in the afternoon, he stopped for a quick beer, the boys waiting outside, patient because they liked the movie, bouncing a ball, and then, after a time, their father came back outside, squinting because it was dark inside the tavern and bright outside. He was not drunk; one at a time on the tab is what he put, only owed the bartender about six bucks. He told the boys that because he had not bought them any popcorn and thought they might be wondering. The semi-pro league was playing ball, and on the way home, they stopped at the field to watch a couple of innings; one of the guys, the catcher, was old, over forty now, but he used to play in the big leagues and he, most times, hit a home run every game in this league. They were not disappointed. He put one clear over the fence, almost into the parking lot of the shopping mall just across the street, a few discount stores. When they passed the hat, the father put in a quarter; it was nearly all he had, but the home run had been worth it. They started for home, the sun just starting to go down, no traffic, quiet on the avenue. He wanted to stop at another place for a beer, but resisted, the lighted beer advertisement blinking in the window just as he passed; his friend Joe worked there and would surely give him one on the house; next time, he thought. The kids wanted pizza from the place where the teenagers hung out listening to the jukebox—big, flat pizzas with thin crusts and a good selection of soda, but he had to tell them no; anyway Martha would be cooking. The boys didn't whine about it, but walked on. He stopped in the church to light a candle, worried about his mother's health, and the boys prayed for their grandmother, noticing the tear just inside their father's eye, not coming out, and they assumed she was dying, but they didn't ask. They crossed themselves with holy water on the way out.

When they got home there was Rice-A-Roni on the stove and the boys complained a little because they had it last night, but their parents figured they didn't understand about budgets, so they didn't explain. There was little good on TV, only repeats in the summer so they didn't watch, not even any good cop shows they wouldn't mind seeing twice, so they played with toy soldiers, playing together pretty well for brothers, whining a little again when they couldn't go to sleep at a friend's house who called too late and whose parents said they'd take them all to an amusement park in the morning, but there wasn't enough money for that and they couldn't very well ask the other boy's parents to pay. There were no questions about why Daddy didn't go to work anymore, they liked having him around. Anyway he wouldn't have known what to tell them and neither did she, although she was starting to get angry, but really didn't deep-down blame him, so couldn't and didn't tell him how she felt. The bickering crept up on them slowly like a fire that's hard to start. She got so she put the want ads at his place at the breakfast table in the morning, and put the rest of the paper somewhere else, in the bathroom even, to hide it, but he'd put the ads aside and ask for the sports page, so even though she said nothing, she stomped her feet when she walked and banged the dishes in the sink loudly to let him know she didn't approve, which he ignored and ignored her, but remained good to the boys, taking them with their baseballs to the park, and stopping only occasionally for a beer with the guys on the way home, which the boys didn't mind and didn't tell their mother, even though they knew the tab was now over twenty dollars because he told them, having to tell someone.

One day, the city work crews came to cut down the trees that had stood and swayed on the street since their father had bought the house, still single, some twenty years before, and before the boys were born, long before. He got mad and started yelling at the workers, and they yelled back, and he yelled some more, and then he went outside to pick a fight, grabbing their tools and still yelling. Then the police came to break it up, and he was mad at Martha because she had called the police, wanting to avoid real trouble, to stop it just it time. The boys were mad at Martha, too, because she had kept them inside and out of trouble when they had wanted to go outside and help their father, but they got over it soon enough and all went out for hamburgers, got away from the noise of the saws.

The good days seemed to stop suddenly like a train, and they stopped going to the park to play ball, while he sat on the couch, watching television, and Martha, their mother, got louder about cooking and doing dishes to the point of breaking some plates, and he'd yell, and she'd yell, and the boys tried to pretend they didn't hear her, disappointed.

When finally they moved from that house and away from that neighborhood, he didn't come with them, but didn't stay either, and went someplace else. The boys started asking questions, of her, not of him, and she couldn't answer them, distraught, but he was gone and they weren't, and they didn't like the new place. The silence was useless and unprotective. They didn't like the new guy she let live with them, but didn't say anything, not being accustomed to it, and she either, and they grew up, became teenagers, still playing baseball, played on their high school team that won a cross-town championship, always two years apart and getting older, seeing their father most weekends. He didn't seem so depressed as at first, working now again, still seeing him even after the home run hitter retired, nearly fifty, from the semi-pro league. All the changes inarticulate as rust.

Light Eater

DENISE'S APARTMENT IS dimly lit and sparsely furnished. It is on the third floor of a building with mostly subsidized tenants.

She is reading to Tommy when the doorbell rings.

"Who's that, Mommy?"

"Just a minute, honey."

Denise gets up to buzz the intercom.

"Denise?"

"I'll be right down."

Denise goes back to the couch, leans down and kisses her son. She grabs a sweater and kisses Tommy again.

"Are you going out again, Mom?"

"I have a date, sweetie."

"Again?"

"I'll be home early. I promise."

"Can we finish 'Thomas the Tank Engine?'"

"My friend is waiting."

"Just a little more? Please!"

"OK. One more page. To right here." Denise points to the end of the page.

"Can you make me dinner before you go?"

"I'll make you dinner when I get home."

"That will be late. I'll be really hungry."

"I'll get home as soon as I can, sweetie. Terry next door will look in on you."

Denise runs out the door before her son can say anything else.

* * *

Robert is standing outside her apartment building by the doorbells and the rows of mailboxes. He is a short man and he is tossing his car keys from hand to hand. This is Denise's second date with him. It is sprinkling lightly on a May evening, late for rain in Los Angeles.

"What took you so long?" Robert is trying to sound unperturbed.

"I was reading to Tommy."

"You didn't want to let me in?"

"It makes it harder on him."

"OK. Where do you want to go?"

"I don't know."

They get into Robert's car, a Chevy Lumina. The radio is on loud, KROQ. Without Denise's asking, Robert turns the volume down.

As soon as the music is quiet, she adds quickly:

"How about the Neapolitan?"

"The portions there are large."

"You like it there?"

The Neapolitan is a Southern Italian place near Hollywood Boulevard and Vermont. Flamboyant gays from Silver Lake mingle with scenesters from East Hollywood and wannabe rock stars. Denise used to go there a lot before she had Tommy.

Robert changes the station to Cool Jazz, smooth sounds.

"If you don't, we can go somewhere else."

"No, no. The Neapolitan's fine. You must be hungry. Those portions are huge."

"I like the atmosphere."

"It's a great place to people-watch."

"That's why I like it.

Robert turns on the windshield wiper as the rain begins to fall harder. Small drops of rain leak through the poorly sealed window and onto Denise.

"Turn up the radio, Robert. Please. I love this song."

Robert turns up the volume and Denise begins to sing along:

"Walking in rhythm,

Moving in sound;

Thinking about my baby,

Trying to move on."

* * *

There is a wait at the Neapolitan. Fifteen to twenty minutes. Not bad for a Saturday night, really—but Denise starts to fidget. Robert notices her anxiety, but tries to be cool.

They give out free wine at the Neapolitan, and Robert wants to wait for a booth, but when the host asks what kind of table they want, Denise says, "First available."

They get seated in less than 15 minutes, but they are stuck in a corner.

Denise orders a large portion of Chicken Parmigiana, a salad, a side of spaghetti with plain tomato sauce and extra garlic bread.

"Boy, you are hungry."

"It all looks so good."

Robert orders a small Veal Marsala.

When the waitress leaves, Denise leans across the table and strokes Robert's hands. He has nice hands, smooth and well shaped.

When the meal arrives, Denise eats hardly anything. She looks at her watch often.

"Are you OK?"

"I'm fine. Really."

Denise continues to pick at her food.

The waitress comes over.

"Are you finished?"

"I'll take all this to go."

"You want the bread?"

"Yeah, everything. Please."

As the waitress leaves, Sal comes over. He is the owner.

"Hey, I haven't seen you in a long time," he says in a thick Sicilian accent. He leans over and kisses Denise on both cheeks.

"I have a small son."

"Out for the night, a little break?"

"Oh, I mean, yeah. And, Sal, this is Robert. Robert, Sal. He owns the place."

"Great food," Robert says as he extends his hand to shake.

"Hey, I'll send over some spumoni," Sal says. He winks at Denise.

Sal sends over both the dessert and the accordion player. He does 'Volare' and 'That's Amore.'

Denise fidgets badly.

Robert passes the musician a five-dollar tip, and he plays on. Robert was not trying to get more songs out of him.

Denise takes the ice cream to go, too.

"I guess my eyes were bigger than my stomach."

"Just a little," Robert says, but affectionately.

"My mother always used to say that." Denise says.

"You want to go someplace for a nightcap?" Robert asks. "The Dresden, maybe?"

"I really have to go home."

"OK."

Robert pays the check. Denise feels she should explain.

"I'm just worried about Tommy," she says. "The babysitter fell through, and my neighbor's looking in on him, but still."

"I understand. I'll take you home."

"Thank you, Robert. I really appreciate it. I really do."

Denise never had a babysitter lined up. She couldn't afford one. Not tonight. Not soon.

Robert drives her straight home.

"Do you want any of this food?" Denise asks outside her apartment. I ordered so much."

"No, you take it."

"Thank you, Robert. I had a great night. I really did. I mean, I know you might not think so, from how nervous I was and everything, but it was really nice."

"Me, too." Robert says and leans over to kiss her.

She leans into him and kisses him long and hard and deep with her tongue. Then she pulls away.

"I've got to go."

"I understand," Robert says for the second time.

She opens the car door and steps out into the rain.

"Next Saturday?"

"OK."

Denise shuts the door, waves briefly, and runs up the stairs.

Upstairs, Tommy is sleeping on the couch, the television still on. Terry has left a note saying she has gone home to bed, but that Tommy had fallen asleep and was fine. She had put the time on her note. It was only half an hour ago.

Denise wakes Tommy up.

"Look, sweet pea. I brought your favorite dinner. Wake up, honey!"

Tommy stirs and wakes up slowly. Denise turns off the TV.

"Hi, Mommy," Tommy says. "I'm so hungry"

"I know, sweetie. But I have chicken and spaghetti and garlic bread and ice cream."

"I was watching 'Nick at Nite.'"

"I know, honey, but it's late. The show is over."

Denise rushes to the kitchen to heat up the food. Tommy eats the spumoni first while she is out of the room.

"Eat all this, honey. It's good."

Tommy eats all the rest of the chicken and the bread and the pasta.

When he is done, he is sleepy again, groggy from a big meal. Denise carries him to her bed where he usually sleeps. She sings to him and soon hears him sleeping soundly. She waits there a few minutes listening to Tommy's rhythmic breathing and to her own stomach growling. "Walking in rhythm, moving in sound." Donald Byrd. She sings the tune a second time.

Quietly she gets up and walks back out to the living room and looks at the paper plate from which her son has eaten, and she peers inside the take-out boxes. He has eaten it all. She goes out to the kitchen and looks in the refrigerator. There is a jar of peanut butter. She gets a tablespoon and scoops it straight from the jar. There is not much left, but scoops it clean. When she is done she goes back to their one bedroom and gets into the queen-size bed beside her son and tries to go to sleep.

Soy Hombre

It was palpably hot. The sun seemed to splatter on the sidewalk like an egg dropped from a third floor window.

She walked barefoot across the pavement. She was pretty and she was carrying a baby in her arms.

The minister watched her and wondered if the soles of her feet were burning. Her legs were long and thin.

The minister sat at his desk. He looked at the woman. And at the others outside and down below through the window of his second floor study. He was preparing his sermon.

Downstairs the woman joined a long line in the courtyard. The church was handing out baby formula and free Pampers to poor and homeless mothers. The minister had started the program just a month ago. He was proud of it and of his congregation who volunteered to work at it so readily.

The church was in a good neighborhood that bordered on a bad one. That is how the Church Board described it to the minister when they hired him. Similar to so many communities in Los Angeles, they had said at his interview.

The pastor closed his Bible and straightened the papers on his desk. It was time to go home. He called his wife to tell her he was on his way. He looked out the window once again. The barefoot woman was now third in line for the baby supplies.

Before going downstairs to lock the doors, the minister reached for a Kleenex from a stylish and manly blue box at the far right corner of his desk. He took one, used it, threw it away, then reached for another. There were no more. He thought about how he never anticipated running out of tissues, how the box seemed, until it was completely empty, to be infinite and unending. He knew that he thought about the world

that way, not just heaven and earth, but everything—his tenure at the church, sex, an afternoon at the beach. He rarely thought about the next thing, or about the end of things. Only the infinite now.

He took a small notebook from the pocket of his sport jacket. He wrote the word "Kleenex" on a shopping list that he had made on the first page of the small, wire-bound pad—right below "grape jelly." He put the notebook back in his pocket.

On the first floor, the paid staff had left. The minister checked the doors, locking those that had been carelessly left open. His receptionist nearly always forgot to lock her door on her way out. He often reminded her that some of the most expensive equipment in the church was in her office—a computer, a copy machine, the scanner, the fax. To no avail. The pastor shook his head to himself and continued to check for unlocked doors.

He had run through nearly his whole routine when the custodian approached him. He spoke rapidly and rose on the balls of his feet when he talked.

"Pastor Reynolds," he said. "There's a man in the courtyard. He's pulling up weeds and grass, and he's talking to himself."

The minister put his keys in his pocket and went outside to see what was going on. In the doorway, he squinted into the sun. He had left his sunglasses on his desk upstairs. His eyes took a minute to adjust. As the custodian had said, a complete stranger was pulling weeds in the courtyard. The man was Latino, about 30, thin and unshaven. Despite the heat, he wore a flannel shirt, buttoned all the way to the top.

The man was saying the same thing over and over. His words were softly spoken. The minister moved closer in order to hear him.

"See," said the janitor. "See what I mean."

The minister was close enough now. He spoke Spanish and Korean, had taken both languages in college and in graduate school. He spoke both languages during the course of his pastoral duties. Here, he could hear the man clearly and he could understand him.

"Soy hombre," the man said. "Puedo trabajar. Soy hombre. Puedo trabajar." He said it again and again as he worked on the weeds.

"Should I call the police?" the custodian asked.

The minister looked at the custodian. He tried to imagine the world as his janitor might see it. He tried to compare it to his own view. He paused for a long time, thinking.

"Pastor?"

"Let him alone, Bob," Pastor Reynolds said. "He's not crazy. He'll leave soon, I imagine."

"He's scaring the ladies in line," Bob said.

The minister looked over at the line of women. He saw the barefoot woman. She had just picked up her pampers and milk and now she was leaving, heading for the bus stop. She held her baby tightly in one arm, the bag of supplies in the other.

It was an evening in July, six o'clock and still hot. The grass on the church grounds was brown and wilted from the heat and the drought.

The woman was wearing a tank top and cut-off jeans, frayed at the ends. Her legs and arms and feet were tanned. She walked quickly.

The pastor looked at the janitor and looked at the woman. He brushed back his hair, which was a little long, slightly gray, and in his eyes. Abruptly, he stepped in front of the woman and put his arms around her and kissed both her and her child.

"Everything will be alright," he said. "It will all work out. Trust me."

The woman kissed him on the cheek.

"Thank you, Pastor," she said. "Thank you. We appreciate what you're doing here."

He held her tightly and for a long time. He felt the sweat running down his neck and back and the damp cotton of her top. He looked up at the treetops, finally beginning to sway in a breeze that had just begun, and then down at her hair, blonde but dark at the roots.

The woman shrugged her shoulders, adjusting her hold on her baby, to distract his embrace.

"I've got tot get going, Reverend," she said.

"Yes, of course. I'm sorry," he said, letting go of her.

"No, not at all," she said. "Thanks again."

The woman walked away, once again moving quickly.

The minister turned to his janitor.

"Bob, could you check the locks tonight?" His tone was unusually humble and plaintive.

"Sure, Pastor. Sure thing."

Without going back upstairs to his office for his briefcase or his sunglasses, the minister headed for his car, a brand new and dark green Chevy Caprice. A nice solid car. He jiggled his keys in his hand as he walked, slowly. When he reached his car he leaned against it and took two pictures from his wallet. One was a picture of a blonde and barefoot woman with long, thin legs; the other, a picture of his wife and son. In the picture the boy is dressed in a Little League uniform. His wife has her dark hair tied back. They are both smiling broadly. As he looked at the pictures, Pastor Reynolds did not smile, but looked without distraction at the photos for a long time. The sun was going down. It was finally cooling off. He put both pictures back in his wallet and walked on and past his car to the bus stop. He checked his watch and slouched against the sign pole, waiting for the bus he had long wanted to take.

The Bracelet

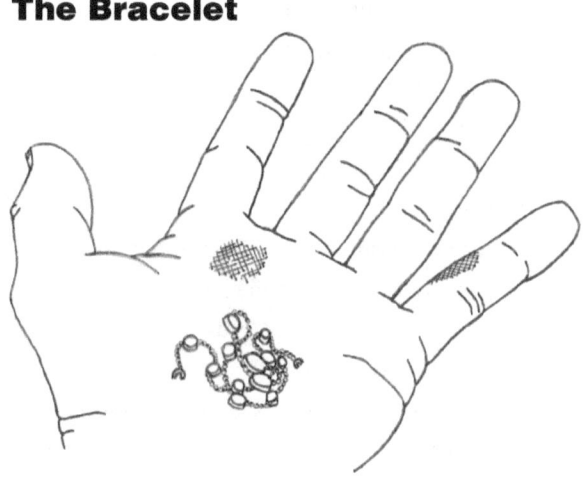

I GIVE THE man a dollar and maybe a little more change.

"I bet he goes out and buys beer with that," my wife says.

"I don't care what he buys with it," I say.

We go through this all the time. I hand out a lot of money on the streets. Not a lot of money, really. I hand out a little bit of money lots of times.

"I don't understand that," she says.

"I know you don't."

I don't want to talk about it. We're going to dinner and a movie, on Vermont Avenue in East Hollywood. We're early for the scene. The scene will come later, after the movie, at the clubs.

The man did seem drunk or high.

"I just don't believe you think about it," she says.

"That's not fair," I say. "If nothing else, if they ask, they must need it more than I do."

"You're not really helping them," she says.

"I know that."

My wife looks good in her orange and green vintage Pucci jacket. She is carrying a blue Prada purse with short handles. I bought them both for her.

It is windy in March and she gathers her collar around her neck. I put my arm around her. I am wearing a thin cardigan sweater. We are in our mid-thirties and we go to lots of nightclubs and we have a good time around here. We are both attorneys for non-profit organizations. We have no children—yet. We eat out a lot.

It has just turned dark. We are out earlier than we usually are because of the movie.

"They need a job," she says.

"Who's going to give them a job?"

"You act like I don't care."

"I know you do," I say.

"Even if I thought about it the way you do, what's a little change going to do?"

"Maybe I'm just salving my own conscience…" I take my arm off her shoulder.

"I didn't say that."

"I know."

"And I know you care…"

"Whatever…"

"Figaro or Vermont?" She asks about the restaurant. Both are expensive; both are my choices, my favorites on the street.

"You can't do nothing," I say.

"I think it makes it worse," she says.

"Let's go to Vermont," I say. It is the more expensive of the two.

As we are talking, the man I gave the money to—maybe a dollar-and-a-half, at most, some coins and a bill—is running up behind us.

"Excuse me," he says, out of breath. "Excuse me."

Now that I look at him more closely, he seems quite looped actually/in fact. He is very dirty and scraggly.

"See, he's going to ask for something else," my wife says.

The man walks up to my wife, not to me. She is not scowling; her face is open; she is ready to listen. He is standing right in front of her. He opens his hand.

"I think you dropped this," he says.

He is holding my wife's bracelet. It is a silver bracelet, with turquoise and coral and amethyst and onyx. I gave it to her last Christmas.

He hands her the bracelet.

She looks at me and I look at her.

The man turns to leave.

My wife says nothing. The man says nothing. I say nothing.

After a minute, she yells "thank you" at his receding back.

My wife and I cross the street to go to dinner. I take her arm again. She puts the bracelet in her purse.

"I'll have to get the clasp fixed," she says.

The man walks away, without turning around, back to where he was standing before, in front of the Bank of America.

The three of us, like packages mailed to different places—some sharing part of a route, others shipped off alone—head off into our nights and the evening is over.

Temporary Reparations

Poz AND Army and their friends ran down the street, rocks clenched tightly in their hands, shouting insults at the top of their lungs.

The sound of the window glass shattering reminded Poz of his mother's last fight with her boyfriend when he trashed the house—breaking vases, plates, dishes. Poz hated it.

The woman who lived in the house poked her head through one of the broken windows and shouted out in Spanish.

After all his friends had gone home, Poz went to the Mexican family's house. He bit his nails and knocked on the door. He had $75 in his pocket—profit from a stolen laptop he had just sold.

When the woman answered the door, Poz said, "I just broke your window and I want to pay for it."

The woman spoke no English so she went to get her son to translate. The kid was only about eight. The woman seemed puzzled when Poz told her what he wanted—she asked her son to say it twice—but she took the money.

Poz walked out and looked around nervously, making sure no one saw him. It wasn't the last time he did something like that, and for a short time his crew broke the family's windows often. Eventually, the Mexicans moved out of the neighborhood.

The Horses of Instruction

WE LAUGHED LOVINGLY when she fell off the horse. We didn't realize she had hurt herself. It was only a pony. Not high off the ground.

That morning a tramp had broken into our car. Right outside the house. The fir trees in front of our place were sculpted like missiles. I never liked that. And furthermore, they obscured our view of the car, which had been stolen several times. I always wanted to cut those trees down, but I was afraid the landlord would evict us for it. He often bragged how nice they looked. Anyway, when I caught the tramp and grabbed him by the collar, he was holding—clenched tightly in his hand—a pack of Peppermint Lifesavers, which had been left sitting on the front seat. He said only that he had been craving a Peppermint Lifesaver and that he couldn't afford one. I gave him a few dollars out of my pocket and told him to get lost. For the rest of the morning, I was sullen and grouchy.

Diana was nine. Every Sunday we drove from the house with the missile firs, which we'd rented for sixteen years, to Griffith Park to take her horseback riding. Diana enjoyed it, and we somehow took satisfaction that we were giving her a privilege—though it was a public riding stable—that we otherwise couldn't afford. Riding was something that seemed beyond our means, but not beyond Diana. We had high expectations of her. She had walked and talked at an early age. Her grandparents said she'd be a genius. No other kid in the neighborhood knew how to ride a horse. Nancy and I were satisfied with our pretension, and Diana seemed to really enjoy it. Not like kids whose parents force them to take piano or ballet. She liked horses. And we liked taking her, each for our own reasons.

That morning, however, after the incident with the tramp, I didn't want to go to the stable. Nancy had given in to my mood. It was Diana who insisted.

We live in a small cul-de-sac off Riverside Drive—between Los Angeles and Glendale. The Los Angeles River is two blocks away, imbedded in concrete and flowing only during wet winters, each about four years apart.

Most of our neighbors work at the better paying blue collar jobs—as I do. Lately, however, there have been a lot of lay-offs—airlines, auto plants, etc. Some of our friends have recently lost their homes to bank foreclosures. Richer people are moving in—architects, lawyers, and the like. I'd rather my old neighbors. Most of my neighbors—these recent young professionals aside—are Latino. Until the foreclosures, we were the only whites on the block, which was fine with me. I knew everyone who lived here and we liked each other. But, I can't see myself getting along with lawyers, or architects for that matter. All their kids probably know how to ride a horse already.

Diana hit her head in the fall. She seemed to forget things. Our laughs turned to concern. The attendant looked in her eyes and told us she'd be all right. So we drove home, skipping a trip to the hospital.

My wife had worked as a belly-dancer at a Greek place in the Valley. On the way home, I wanted to know if we could go there sometime soon. Get a babysitter. Maybe next Saturday night. Nancy was worried about Diana, who was quiet all the way home. Nancy said no, we couldn't go there. Not any more. The place had changed hands. She was irritated with me for suggesting it. I was thinking of Diana too, but I wasn't saying what I was thinking. That was the beginning.

For weeks, we worried about brain damage. Mostly me. Nancy had relaxed about it. Every time Diana failed a test at school, I got apprehensive. Why did we listen to the attendant? Yet even Diana said she was all right. But she was only nine. And she was so uncharacteristically quiet. We should have taken her to the doctor anyway. We finally did, several weeks later, and they hooked electrodes to her head, and several hours later, said she was okay.

I was never satisfied.

The tramps appeared more frequently on our doorstep as time went by. I did less and less to get rid of them. Let the lawyers take care of the problem.

I began to go to séances. I didn't tell Nancy. I thought somehow that the dead might know if Diana's brain had been truly damaged. I did all sorts of crazy things. I really wanted to know.

At the séances, I was in the company of a group of people who, up until now, I would have considered crazies. Nuts, or whatever you want to call them. Unstable people.

I had responded to an ad in the paper, one of those local weeklies aimed at college kids. A Mrs. Torrance answered the phone. Tuesday night at seven-thirty and the address; that's all I could I could get out of her. I'd have to show up at the séance to find out anything about the methods or the content, she said. The 'spirits' wouldn't approve of her telling me anything more over the telephone.

When I arrived the first night, after telling Nancy I was going out to play cards with some old friends, several weird-looking people were already seated in a circle on pillows in Mrs. Torrance's living room. I wondered what Mr. Torrance thought about all of this. I later learned Mrs. Torrance was a widow.

Mrs. Torrance—she said I could call her Edna, but at first I refused—led me to my pillow. The new person was always assigned the same spot, just to the left of the séance leader—Mrs. Torrance, as it turned out.

As the séance was about to begin, the sense of mission that had driven me there left me altogether. I was my old cynical self again, on the verge of cracking a joke, and for that moment, my compulsion about Diana's fall was non-existent. When the lights went out, it soon returned.

The crazies understood my predicament, and I liked them for that. But, after talking with several deal people at several sessions, all of us bathed in a red light that seemed more befitting a brothel, I learned nothing about the condition of Diana's brain.

During the nights following Diana's accident—in the awful quiet dark—I heard the city's noises. I could not sleep. In those days, they had not yet closed the fire station. (Tax cutting measures would soon take care of that. We would be involved in the neighborhood's protest of the station's closing.) The sound of the sirens and of the loud roar of the big fire truck engines were noises to which I had long become accustomed. Yet, at that time, even the most familiar of sounds woke me or kept me awake. My tossing and turning soon drove Nancy to ask me to sleep on the couch. I was disturbing her sleep. We did not have an extra bedroom. I understood, and spent most of the nights during the next several months sleeping—or not—on the narrow sofa, even once tossing and turning so violently that I rolled off onto the floor. I hurt my ribs in the fall. Soon the insomnia passed, but still I was beset by Diana's problems—or the problems of my imagination, whichever you choose.

It took me several months to sleep through the night. It was then I took to shooting horses. I bought a revolver—cheap—a "Saturday Night Special," as they call it. One night a week, usually Friday, I would sneak out late and drive to the stable where Diana had ridden. She had given up riding in favor of clothes and records and that sort of thing. The drive at night up through the dark woods that marked the approach to the Equestrian Center, past the skating rink, and on into what seemed to my city eyes a real wilderness, persuaded me somehow of the glory of my mission.

The horses were kept in a barn for the night. The barn was padlocked with a cheap lock, which I pried open with the tire iron stored in my trunk. As soon as I pushed the door open, the smell hit me. I was born and raised in the city. The country had always given me the creeps. As I stepped into the barn, my eyes adjusting to the dark, the odor stuck in my throat, I coughed and the horses began to shuffle nervously. I was surprised that any of them were awake.

I stopped at the first stall and turned on my flashlight. The stall was only about two feet longer than the horse that was in it—a tired-looking, dark brown mare—and maybe twice as wide. This horse was awake, standing quietly, a little bit of food—oats, I thought—stuck around her mouth. She carried her head low. I decided she was too vulnerable and sad-looking, and moved on to the next stall. It contained a male horse of a stature beyond what I expected of a public riding stable. He was well-muscled and dark black; he looked more as if he should be racing at Santa Anita (or Hollywood Park). Maybe a bad leg had brought him here. I didn't care.

I took the gun in two hands like a matinee detective, crouched, and pulled the trigger three times. The horse snorted, shot its head upward, thrashed loudly against the wooden stall, then sank to the ground. I left quickly, but not nervously.

Three weeks later, I would shoot the pathetic mare.

I am still not sure what finally made me stop, but before I was through, I had killed four horses.

Last year, our oldest boy, John, was arrested in Italy, for bombing a bank.

Diana graduated from Stanford magna cum laude, which they tell me means "high honors" in Latin.

She's twenty-three now, and the fall from her horse has seemingly caused her to do nothing weird.

Last week, Diana took a job as a pathology assistant with the County Coroner's Office. She works with the dead.

Scrap Metal

THERE IS A MAN walking along the train tracks on Alameda Street. He is dirty. He is picking up cans and putting them in a green plastic bag.

Is he working hard or is he a bum?

I stop to talk to him. He will take the metal and the glass to a center, he says. They will pay him for the stuff, he tells me.

Is he a scavenger or an entrepreneur?

"Do you have any?" he asks me.

"What?" I say at first.

He stops to pick up a can. It is a Miller Lite can and it is crushed.

"It's still good," he says.

"Maybe I do," I say, and I fish out my keys and point to my car.

It is hot; I can feel the heat coming from the metal of the tracks. My shirt dots with sweat. There is litter everywhere. The trash does not move because there is no wind.

Inside my car it is still cool because of lingering effects of the air conditioner. I feel around on the floor of the back seat and find five empty Diet Pepsi cans. He smiles when I hand them to him.

He smiles again when I offer him a ride.

Is he grateful or just glad he doesn't have to walk?

We drive all the way up Alameda to 7th Street. The Central City Recycling Center sits on a full city block. Piled two stories high are bales of compressed newspaper and cardboard, bound with metal wire. They look like packages waiting to be mailed. He squints and nods and gets out of the car.

"Gracias," he says, "Goodbye."

"I'll wait," I say.

He seems puzzled, but he picks up his bag of cans and closes the car door. He nods again through the window. I leave the engine on so the car will stay cool. There is a small puddle of liquid on the floor of the passenger side where he put his bag down. I get a paper towel from the glove compartment to soak it up. I notice new dirt on the upholstery, but there is nothing I can do about that now. I turn on the radio.

When he returns, he shows me what he's got in his hand. I count it with him: $12.40.

"Mucho dinero," he says. "Mucho dinero."

I offer to take him for a beer. He smiles again.

Is he happy about the situation or does he just smile a lot?

We go to a Mexican bar on San Julian. He introduces me to his friends. I buy them all a beer. It is cheap. He singles out his best friend, who tells me he is an astronaut.

"Soy astronaut, señor," are his exact words.

"Si, si," I say and smile.

I tell him about my divorce and my job. He tells me about Mercury, Gemini, and Apollo.

I turn back to the first guy and ask him more about collecting can and bottles, questions like: how much do the recycling centers pay and where are the best places to find a lot of cans.

We drink until very late when the bar closes. We are quite drunk and I have spent most of my money. He has spent none of his so far that I know, which is fine with me. It is the way I planned it.

We make arrangements to meet again.

Is he my friend now, or just another somebody else that I really don't want to know?

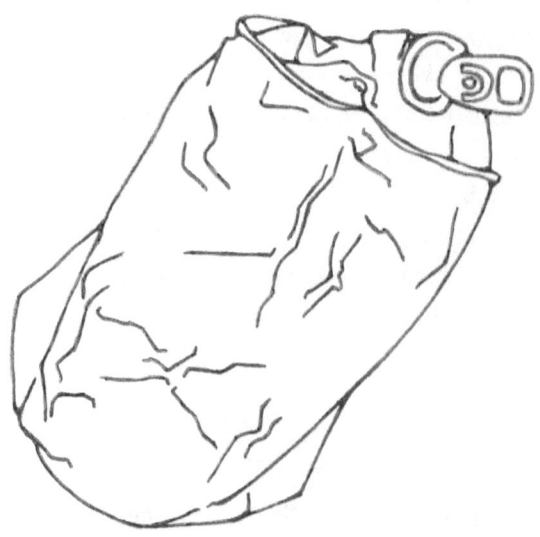

Dirtier

I WAS DIRTY; she was dirtier.

We crawled into her cardboard box.

I had our bottle of Night Train.

Albert had the biggest tent. His friend told me he'd saved his SSI checks for two months, quit smoking and drinking, so he could pay for it.

All the parties, big and small, were in Albert's tent. And, he got all the girls downtown.

I would find her there sometimes.

* * *

Inside her box, we lit some candles.

When I rubbed the back of her neck, I could feel the grease and the sweat—weeks' worth of accumulation roiling under my fingertips.

Some of her nails were long and some were short. The cuticles were rimmed in black on the short ones; the long ones had grime caked under the length of them like dirt stuck on a shovel. She took my shirt off and her long nails scratched me. I could feel them part the rivulets of my sweat as she darted them along and around my shoulders, my back and my chest. I was very hard.

I took her hands in mine and I sucked her filthy fingers one by one, varying the pressure of my lips and tongue. She began to moan softly. I unbuttoned the top of her jeans and unzipped her.

I'd only been out on the streets about a month. All's I had was a bedroll—no tent, no box, nothing to sleep in. I found doorways and alleys.

Then Albert started letting me sleep in his tent from time to time.

Sometimes she was there.

* * *

They were remodeling a storefront at 4th and Main. I asked a construction worker what it would be, and he said they were opening a bar. That's cool, I thought.

When they were finished, I wandered over there. It was full of rich people. I strolled back to the King Eddie.

* * *

She was very dirty and she smelled very strong and when I slipped her pants off she smelled even stronger. I pulled off her shoes; she wasn't wearing any socks. Her feet were filthy, too, of course, and the smell of her feet mingled with the smell of her pussy and her ass in the candlelit box we were fucking in. I began sucking on her toes, then licked up her calves, and back down to her feet. By the time I let my tongue linger along her thighs, then went down on her for good, she was dripping wet.

* * *

Putting up a tent is faster than taking it down. That's what Albert told me. Joey agreed.

On Los Angeles Street, the person who pitches their tent next to you is your neighbor. Sometimes they choose you day after day, always getting the space beside you. Albert and Joey were always next to each other.

"He's got my back," Albert said.

People sometime got jealous of Albert because he had such a nice tent.

Joey always defended him.

"He saved up for that tent."

Nobody got jealous of Joey, but they listened to him.

Joey had the smaller tent.

* * *

Our box was on 2nd Street by the shuttered and empty St. Vibiana's Cathedral, the new Catholic temple under construction just a few miles away.

Back then 2nd Street was boxes; Los Angeles Street was tents.

I licked her fast and then slow, hard and soft and she came and she screamed when she came.

We could hear the laughter and the catcalls coming form the boxes alongside hers.

I drank in her odors and I was about to come just from eating her out.

After a bit, she held my head at bay, taking a break, and I licked her soiled stomach, which was surprisingly taut.

She rolled me over and climbed on top of me. I was so excited I had to slow down her thrusts.

She bounced gently on me for a time, then she let go.

The Night Train finally kicked in, calming me down. I breathed slowly and I followed her rhythm and I held onto my orgasm.

The box was big—I don't know what came in it, something larger than a refrigerator—and she was springing up and down so violently on my cock that she kept hitting her head on the top of the box.

We didn't laugh then; we laughed later.

We fucked and fucked and then I shot up hard inside her. I was quiet as I came because I was used to that and I held her and she looked in my eyes for assurance and I assured her with my eyes and she stuck her fingers back in my mouth and once again I sucked them one by one.

* * *

I found a newspaper in the trash and I read it.

The downtown businesses were telling the City Council that Skid Row was bad for the city, that they should clean up the neighborhood, that we were detrimental to the future of Los Angeles.

I threw the paper back in the garbage.

* * *

She told me her name was Andi and we finished the bottle of Night Train and we smoked the last of our cigarettes and we held our dirty bodies close all day and all night.

* * *

Around dawn the police came and along with them they had trucks from Public Works and they rousted us and they smashed our tents and our boxes and they rounded us up and shoved us against walls and they patted us down, looking for drugs or weapons or whatever else, and they loaded our belongings into the trucks and they carted our stuff away to a dump, to some location, to wherever, never to be seen again.

By noon we'd re-gathered, come together again, those of us remaining, and we tried to reorganize, but we had nothing much left.

Albert's tent was gone and so was Joey's, and all the boxes were gone, including Andi's, and I couldn't see her anywhere, and I looked around, but she wasn't there, so I asked—I asked Albert and Joey and I asked the people without tents on 2nd Street, and no one seemed to know, until one old woman, dirty and disheveled, came over to me as I was calling Andi's name and she said the police had arrested her, had taken her away—they'd found drugs or something on her person, that's how she put it—but, anyway, they'd put her in a patrol car and driven off—they drove away with Andi in the back seat in handcuffs—and I never saw her again.

City Blocks

Broken bottles, shattered glass.
I decry my deciduous life; I molt like a reptile.
Trash swirls and eddies in the gutters like dirty water in a drain.
She holds my hand and lets it go.
I live alone in a single room; last year I did not.
At the dark bar, spilled beer puddles on the polyurethane.
We don't know whether to stay or leave. For a whole host of reasons.
We stay until the pungent end.
I light a cigarette; she does not smoke.
I wander the streets until dawn.
The sun is a binding document.

About the Author

LARRY FONDATION is the author of the novels *Angry Nights* and *Fish, Soap and Bonds*, and of *Common Criminals*, a collection of short stories. His fiction focuses on the Los Angeles underbelly.

His two most recent books feature collaborations with artist Kate Ruth.

Fondation has lived in LA since the 1980s and worked for fifteen years as an organizer in South Central Los Angeles, Compton, and East LA.

His fiction and non-fiction pieces have appeared in a range of diverse publications including *Flaunt* (where he is Writer-at-Large), *Plastique*, *West*, *Fiction International*, *Night Train*, *Quarterly West*, the *Los Angeles Times* and the *Harvard Business Review*. He is a recipient of a 2008-09 Christopher Isherwood Fellowship in Fiction Writing.

He can be contacted at lfondation@aol.com

About the Illustrator

KATE RUTH is an artist who works with many media and in many fields. As a fine artist, Kate both paints and draws. She creates elegant line drawings, often with splashes of color, and her subject matter is as intriguing as her style. Strippers, good-time girls, and denizens of the streets of New York feature prominently in a number of her best-known works. Kate's crisp style and clean lines give all her subjects dignity and beauty. Since 2001, she has published four books of her drawings.

In addition to this work, Kate is a notable stylist and illustrator, with a wide variety of clients, projects and publications. She graduated with Honors in English Literature and Philosophy from Victoria University in 2001.

www.ingramcontent.com/pod-product-compliance
Lightning Source LLC
Chambersburg PA
CBHW050824180626
46814CB00004B/1449